Carry On Loving

*The wickedly funny story that
starts where the film ends*

Norman Giller

Chameleon

For Michael
A son who has taught his father
that life is just a game

First published in Great Britain in 1996 by
Chameleon Books
106 Great Russell Street
London WC1B 3LJ

CIP data for this title is available
from the British Library

ISBN 0 233 99029 1

Typeset by Falcon Oast Graphic Art

Printed in Great Britain by WBC, Bridgend

Author's Acknowledgements

This book could not have been written without the original foundation work of *Carry On* film creators Peter Rogers and Gerald Thomas. I have simply carried on where they left off, but I would not even have managed the first step without their marathon screen productions to inspire me. I am also indebted to the *Carry On* team of actors, who brought their characters to life on screen and turned the film series into a national institution. I acknowledge, too, the lovingly crafted screenplays of the writers, and in particular Talbot Rothwell and Norman Hudis. On behalf of the Publishers, I thank the Rank Organisation for allowing us to step into the *Carry On* territory that has always been exclusive to the silver screen, and for their permission to use still photographs from the original film version of *Carry On Loving*.

My thanks also to VCI Chief Executive Steve Ayres for letting me off the leash, and to Tim Forrester, Tom Rosenthal and John Cleary at Chameleon Books for their encouragement; also to my House Editor Stephanie Goodwin, and to Richard Percy, who first had the brainwave to turn the *Carry On* films into books. Most of all, thanks to Eileenalanna, Lisa and Michael for being there.

The characters and events depicted on the following pages are entirely fictitious, and anybody who wishes to argue otherwise will be laughed out of court. *Carry On Laughing...*

Introduction

This book carries on where the film *Carry On Loving** left off. The story so far:

Sidney and Sophie Bliss (Sidney James and Hattie Jacques) are a husband and wife team who run the Wedded Bliss Matrimonial Dating Agency. They are not exactly the best advertisement for wedded bliss, and spend much of their time at each other's throats like fighting bulldogs.

They arrange dates for their clients by matching them with help from a sophisticated-looking computer. It is in fact worked by hand from an adjoining office. Despite their total incompetence and carelessness, they manage to successfully pair and prepare dozens of couples for marriage.

Their greatest triumph comes when they find a willing partner for Percival Snooper (Kenneth Williams), a

*The classic comedy film *Carry On Loving* is available in the *Carry On* series on Cinema Club videos, distributed by VCI, price £4.99.

marriage guidance counsellor who had always been a sworn bachelor until falling under the spell of man-mad Miss Dempsey (Patsy Rowlands).

Bungling private detective James Bedsop (Charles Hawtrey) is kept busy by Sophie Bliss, with orders to keep hot on the trail of her husband as he continually tries to bring personal comfort and company to the lonely hearts (provided they've got big knockers).

Now, Bernie Biddle (Bernard Bresslaw), Sheila Blige (bearing an uncanny resemblance to Barbara Windsor) and funeral director Ivor Bodie (Kenneth Connor) join in the merry mayhem as the Wedded Bliss dating agency runs into a financial crisis because there is too much free love being given away. 'It's all this flower power stuff,' moans Sidney. 'All you've got to do is wave a bleedin' daffodil under a girl's nose these days and she'll lie on her back for you. Why bother to pay dating agency fees when you can get nookie for a mittful of bloody dandelions.'

So come with the *Carry On* team back to the dawn of the 1970s, just after threepenny bits had disappeared and when LSD stopped meaning pounds shillings and pence. Fasten your seat belts. It could be a bumpy trip.

Now Carry On reading...

1

SINGLE GENTLEMAN, 30ISH, ASSISTANT DIRECTOR, OXBRIDGE EDUCATED, OWN MOTOR, SEEKS FEMALE COMPANION, 20ISH, FOR COUNTRY WALKS, CONCERTS, AND A FRIENDSHIP LEADING TO POSSIBLE MATRIMONIAL BEDDED BLISS. MUST HAVE BIG KNOCKERS. BOX 6792.

SIDNEY BLISS studied his latest work of fiction before preparing to hand deliver it to the local *Evening Advertiser* for inclusion on the lonely hearts page. He felt the familiar blow torch breathing of his wife's dragon breath on the back of his neck as she read the prose over his shoulder.

'You can't say that,' she screeched, reaching over and screwing up the advertisement written on Wedded Bliss Matrimonial Dating Agency notepaper.

'Why not?' protested Sidney. 'It's true.'

'What d'you mean it's true?' said Sophie Bliss, who was Sidney's partner in bed, marriage and the dating agency business. 'We haven't got any Oxbridge-educated clients on our books.'

'Well, you've got to allow a little poetic licence,' he said. 'Our latest client, Bernie Biddle, was at Oxford once.'

'He was?'

'Yeah, on the Cowley conveyor belt fitting the door 'andles on Morris Oxfords.'

'And what's this assistant director bit?'

'Well he is the assistant to a funeral director.'

'That's as maybe,' Sophie said, 'but you can't go talking about big knockers in a newspaper advertisement.'

'But it's a scientifically proven fact that every feller wants a bird with big knockers.'

'What do you mean, scientifically proven?'

'Who was a greater scientist than that Albert Einstein geezer?' said Sidney, truly believing he was making a telling point. 'It was him who said that size is relative. I've 'eard he loved experimenting with big knockers.'

'I don't care what you say,' said Sophie, 'the Wedded Bliss Dating Agency has not sunk so low that it has to resort to using words like knockers and telling lies about a client having his own motor.'

'Well he does, in a manner of speaking.'

'Sidney, you know and I know that Mr Biddle works for the undertakers downstairs and rides a bike.'

'Yes, but he's often allowed to take the hearse he drives home with him.'

'I don't know, Sidney,' said Sophie, flopping down at her desk, 'you really worry me. The older you get the dafter you get. I thought it was women who suffered from the menopause. But I think you're proving that there is a male mid-life crisis.'

'I'll show you what a mid-life crisis is,' said Sidney, bringing out of his desk drawer a pile of unpaid bills and bank statements printed in crimson ink. 'This is a mid-life crisis. Bills that we can't meet and bank statements that pour through the letterbox like a river of blood. I've got bills to the left of me, bills to the right of me and stroppy debt collectors surrounding me.'

8

'I'm sure it's only a temporary blip,' said Sophie, typing out a new small-ad entry for Bernie Biddle. 'Business will soon pick up.'

'Pick up?' snapped Sidney. 'Pick up? There's more chance of me picking up myxomatosis than our business improving.'

'But myxomatosis is a disease that only affects rabbits.'

'Exactly, and that's what's going on out there,' he said, pointing a finger out of the second-floor window overlooking the high street. 'They're all at it like rabbits. The swinging sixties 'ave given way to the psychedelic seventies and everybody's into this free love lark. What chance has a dating agency got when they're bleedin' well *giving* it away.'

He pointed to a front page picture in that morning's paper of hippies leading a protest march against the war in Vietnam. 'Look at the placards they're carrying,' he said. 'Make Love Not War. 'Ow can we compete against that sort of mass advertising? All that flower power stuff and mass LSD-inspired love-ins. Wave a bleedin' daffodil under a girl's nose these days and she'll lie on her back for you. Why bother to pay dating agency fees when you can get your nookie for a mittful of bloody dandelions. Let's get back to the days when LSD meant pounds, shillings and pence and when a feller was prepared to put his hand in his pocket to give a girl a good time. Blimey, now girls are looking to put their hands in *his* pocket to give *him* a good time.'

Sidney made a closer study of the newspaper photograph, and was almost drooling. 'I mean,' he said, 'look at the flipping skirts they're almost wearing. It leaves nothing to the imagination. Much shorter and they would be called belts. And I bet they're all on this bloody new birth pill, too. It's become the "stop me and have one" culture. They're just asking for it, they are. Asking for it.'

'Asking for what?' said Sophie, her concentration centred on typing out the advertisement.

'Oh, you wouldn't know what I'm talking about. *IT*. That's what they're asking for. Something that you've stopped giving.'

'You know the rules, Sidney Bliss,' said Sophie, continuing her heavy two-fingered typing. 'Every time you decide to try to keep one of our lonely hearts company, I fine you by withdrawing your conjugal rights.'

'Do me a favour. We've only got three flipping clients of the opposite gender on our books at the moment and I wouldn't touch any of them with my umbrella let alone any part of my being.'

'Yes, but we would have many more ladies on our books if you didn't frighten them away with your objectionable advances.'

'What we need is some financial advances, or we'll have a date for ourselves in Carey Street.'

He now switched his anger to the radio in the corner of their rented office, which occupied two cramped rooms above a funeral parlour. 'What d'you get when you switch that thing on?' he said. 'The bloody Beatles going on about "All You Need Is Love" or Elvis thrusting his pelvis and warbling "Love Me Tender".

10

The punters are 'aving it shoved down their throats, so to speak, night and day, and they can't wait to get at each other the minute they come out of the office or off the factory floor. Come to think of it, a lot of them are having it in the office and *on* the factory floor'

'You're way out of date, Sidney. Slade have taken over from the Beatles. They're number one at the moment with "Skweeze Me, Pleeze Me".'

'Thank you for making my point. You see, Squeeze Me, Bloody Please Me. There was a time when you had to make a date with a girl to get a squeeze, now it's there for free. It's a groper's bloody paradise out there. Who needs a dating agency?'

Sophie ignored the tirade, and finished typing the new advertisement. 'Here you are, Sidney,' she said. 'Take this next door to the newspaper small-ads department, and on the way back pop in and buy some fish and chips for our lunch. Pay for three lonely heart entries, starting on Thursday.'

'One ruddy entry would be a bonus for me these days,' he grumbled under his breath as he took the advertisement and started to read it on his way downstairs:

GENTLEMAN, EARLY 30S, FUNERAL DIRECTOR'S ASSISTANT, SEEKS COMPANION FOR FRIENDSHIP WITH A VIEW TO FUTURE WEDDED BLISS. HOBBIES CRIBBAGE, DOMINOES, SHOVE-HALFPENNY AND DARTS. WOULD SUIT A LONELY BARMAID. BOX 6792.

Sidney paused on the bottom stair and took out a Biro

11

pen from his inside jacket pocket. He deleted the word
funeral, on the basis that director's assistant sounded
more exciting, and he added the adjective 'buxom'
before barmaid. It was important to try to attract a
barmaid with plenty of pull.

By coincidence, Bernie Biddle was just coming into
the funeral parlour, his huge six foot six inch frame half
hidden by a coffin that he was helping undertaker Ivor
Bodie manoeuvre into the chapel of rest. This was at
the rear of the shop that backed on to a propeller-testing
factory. The noise reverberating through the chapel wall
was often enough to wake the dead.

'Blimey, business is booming for you Mr Bodie,' said
Sidney. 'They're going down like flies.'

'Yes,' said Bodie, his face longer than a weekend in
Ostend and fattened by false teeth that were two sizes
too big for his mouth – rumour had it, he had
"borrowed" them from one of his clients who would
have had no more need for them. 'There's been an
outbreak of a deadly virus at the local hospital. Best
news I've had in years.'

'Any news for me, Mr Bliss?' asked Bernie, as he
turned the occupied coffin up on its end so that Sidney
could squeeze by.

'Give us a chance,' he said. 'You only came on our
books last week. We've run you through the computer,
and we'll be advertising you this week as the bargain of
the month. We're telling prospective dates that you've
got everything in working order and have an engine
that's not been run into the ground. Blimey, we're
talking virgin territory. That's as rare these days as

12

finding a banana without bruises.'

Sidney had reached the door before his parting shot. 'I just hope that when it comes to the moment that matters you can get as stiff as the geezer in that coffin,' he said.

'This is not a geezer,' said Bernie. 'It's Mrs Stoneham.'

'What, the wife of the jeweller across the road?'

'Yes, this is Mrs Stoneham,' said Bernie, all but making a formal introduction. 'Expired yesterday, at the age of ninety-seven.'

'Cor, I remember Charlie Stoneham marrying her for her money twenty years ago,' said Sidney. 'Thought he'd inherit it within a couple of years. She certainly gave him a run for her money.'

He made a mental note to drop an agency dating card into the jewellers' letterbox and then continued on his way to the newspaper office next door.

Sidney was queuing at the small-ad counter when his eye was pleasantly taken by the unmistakeable wiggle-while-you-work walk of *Advertiser* reporter Sheila Blige. She had just come down the spiral staircase that led from the editorial offices on the first floor. It was said that cricked necks had become a common affliction for the men working downstairs in the advertising department, caused by watching Miss Blige wiggle her way up and down the open staircase.

'Now if I could have a client like 'er on the books we would be fighting the customers off,' Sidney thought to himself. He flashed her his brightest, sexiest smile and was amazed to find that for the first time in the six months since she had joined the newspaper she returned it.

He looked over both shoulders just to make sure her smile was not meant for somebody else. As he faced the front again he gulped when he found that the vision of his dreams was not only standing right next to him but was actually talking to him.

'Am I right in thinking you're Mr Bliss, the proprietor of the dating agency next door?' she asked.

'Sidney Bliss, miss,' he said, holding out a hand with a calling card that appeared almost as if by magic from his top pocket. The card, that he had had printed against Sophie's strong objections, read:

WEDDED BLISS MATRIMONIAL

DATING AGENCY

WE FIND THE CATCHES AND MAKE THE MATCHES.

OUR BUSINESS IS YOUR PLEASURE.

DON'T BE LATE, MAKE A DATE AND FIND A MATE.

Prop.: Sidney and Sophie Bliss

Miss Blige glanced at the card and tried hard not to cringe. 'I was wondering if you could spare ten minutes or so for a little chat,' she said. 'I need to talk to you quite urgently.'

True, Sidney would not see forty again but here was proof, if proof was needed, that he still had the old animal attraction that he considered had always made him a dynamic magnet for the opposite sex. It could, after all, only have been animal instincts, he thought, that managed to lure a hard-skinned rhino like Sophie into his life. Now here he was being chatted up by a girl who turned more heads than a Centre Court rally. 'Certainly, uh, Miss, uh...'

'Blige,' she said, holding out a hand. 'Sheila Blige. I'm a news reporter on the *Advertiser*.'

'Really, 'ow interesting,' said Sidney, not letting on that he had found out that fact within minutes of her making her first eye-catching walk down the high street. He remembered the moment well. He had given a piercing wolf whistle out of the open office window just as one of Ivor Bodie's clients was being carried out to the hearse below at the start of the last journey. The whistle would not have been quite so bad had he not immediately followed it by shouting to Bernie, whose head he could make out passing below, 'Makes you feel good to be alive, don't it?' How was he to know that balanced on Bernie's broad shoulders was one corner of the coffin bearing the last remains of the dear departed?

'I'm just dashing out on a job now,' she said. 'But I would like to talk to you in your office when you have time.'

The office? What, with the rhino listening in? 'I'll tell you what,' he said, 'I'll see you in the saloon bar of the Pleasant Pheasant Plucker this evening at seven.'

'Fine,' she said. 'I want to talk to you in confidence about becoming one of your clients.'

She wiggled off in her thigh-high mini-skirt, her buttocks churning like two puppies in a sack.

Sidney was left speechless at the small-ad counter. 'If she wants to become a client,' he thought, 'I'll be the first in there for a date.'

'Can I help you?' the advertising assistant asked.

'Yes, please,' said a stunned Sidney. 'Cod and chips twice, and one gherkin.'

Back at the office, Sophie was getting the home-built 'Date Data Computer' warmed up ready for the arrival of their only would-be client of the day. The computer was as false as Ivor Bodie's teeth. It actually consisted of two gramophone turntables placed on their side eight feet apart and rotating behind a balsa wood facade that Sidney, using elementary carpentry skills, had copied from an old photograph of the control room at Cape Canaveral. A client's card placed in a slot at one end of the 'computer' emerged at the other end after five minutes of turning and churning and flashing lightbulbs. Whirring sound effects were added on an EP record playing in the inner office on the other side of the wall where either Sidney or Sophie would be busily typing in the relevant facts on the card.

Sidney always interviewed the female clients, while Sophie collected details from the males. The one client this day had telephoned for an appointment that morning. He had declined to give his name when Sophie spoke to him, and she put it down to his shyness. She had struggled to hear him because he seemed to be talking in little more than a whisper. All he had said was, 'I need a woman, and I shall call in to see you at two o'clock this afternoon.'

To get to the Wedded Bliss Matrimonial Dating Agency was an ordeal in itself. There were four steep flights of stairs, fifty-two steps in all. Sidney had once counted them to see how many he had fallen down when unwisely leaving the office after downing a bottle of whisky following one of his innumerable arguments with Sophie. The Bliss agency had often lost clients at the halfway point. They would turn and walk back downstairs rather than continue to climb, despite appetite-sharpening arrowed posters that read 'this way for the date of your dreams.'

'One day,' said Sophie, 'we're going to have somebody die on these stairs from lack of oxygen.'

It was Ivor Bodie who had said, 'I do hope so.'

Sidney was in the back office reading *Sporting Life* and daydreaming about his date that evening with the delectable Sheila Blige, while Sophie was sitting out front eating the last of her cod and chips with her fingers out of newspaper when she heard a strange wheezing noise outside the door.

She wiped her fingers on her cardigan and went and opened the door. Stumbling in came a man in his early seventies, who was on the edge of exhaustion after making it to the top of the stairs.

Sophie recognised him immediately. It was Mr Stoneham, the jeweller from across the street. She helped him to a seat in front of her desk, and then went and sat facing him. It was two minutes before he could get a word out.

'I'm Charles Stoneham,' he said through wheezing breath, his chest sounding like an out-of-tune concertina.

'Yes,' said Sophie. 'The jeweller from across the street. How's Mrs Stoneham?'

'Not very well,' said Stoneham, with a glazed look in his eyes. 'In fact, she's dead.'

Sophie was so startled that she involuntarily put her a hand to her mouth. 'Oh dear,' she said. 'I'm so sorry. When did she die?'

'Last night,' he said. 'And about bloody time.'

Sophie tried to pretend she had not heard that last sentence.

'Was it, uh, sudden?'

'Sudden?' he said, with a surge of breath brought on by agitation. 'Sudden? I've been waiting for the old cow to go for twenty years.'

Sophie moved uncomfortably in her seat. 'I see, Mr Stoneham,' she said, putting on her professional face. 'And how can the Wedded Bliss Dating Agency help you?'

'As I told you on the telephone this morning, I want a woman,' he said.

'Fine,' said Sophie. 'Well, that's what we're here for... to bring the lonely hearts of this world together.'

She took out a file card and prepared to make handwritten notes. 'Is there any particular sort of lady you have in mind?'

'Well, she's got to be a good cook...'

'Good cook,' Sophie said as she noted it down.

'It would be handy if she could drive...'

'A driver...'

'She mustn't cackle too much...'

'Quite,' said Sophie, 'A quiet lady...'

'She mustn't be afraid of a little housework...'

'Good housekeeper,' Sophie noted.

'And some shop counter experience would help...'

'Counter assistant-type...'

'She needs to be considerably younger than me...'

'Younger lady who likes older men...'

'Oh yes, and she must have big knockers.'

Sidney, looking on through a slot in the "computer" grid, hugged himself and gave a suppressed laugh. 'Another triumph for science,' he said to himself. 'Good old Albert Einstein.'

Trying hard to keep the look of disgust and disdain off her face, Sophie stood up to show that the interview was over. 'Well, Mr Stoneham, I shall feed your details into our computer at a later date. I am afraid it is down at the moment.'

She wanted him out of the office as quickly as possible, and she would fumigate the place the minute he had gone.

'I won't be able to meet her until after the funeral,' Stoneham said.

'Out of respect to the late Mrs Stoneham, of course,' said Sophie.

'Oh no,' he said. 'I'm having the lads round and we're going to have a week-long booze up.'

As Sophie opened the door for him, she wondered about pushing him down the stairs.

Sidney was waiting for her as she turned back into the office. 'You soppy Sophie,' he said, something that had started out as a term of endearment when they first got married but which was now a rebuke. 'You forgot to ask him for a deposit.'

Before Sophie could reply there was a loud thumping

sound coming from the stairs.

The Blisses got jammed together in the door as they both tried to get out at the same time. When they finally extricated themselves and got to the top of the stairs they looked down to see Mr Stoneham lying at the bottom of the second flight, with Ivor Bodie hovering over him like a vulture.

The funeral director looked up, his long face almost radiant. 'He's had a heart attack,' he said, his teeth making what sounded like a death rattle. 'I shall make immediate arrangements for a double burial.'

Sidney looked at the poster above the now deceased Charlie Stoneham's body: THIS WAY FOR THE DATE OF YOUR DREAMS.

'I just hope the poor old sod gets his wish up there,' he said to Sophie, who pulled a face and shuddered.

'If Mrs Stoneham gets her hands on him,' she said, 'she'll kill him.'

2

T HE FIRST RULE for regulars at the Pleasant Pheasant Plucker was that on arrival they had to hand their car keys to landlord George Drinkwater. Then, on leaving, he would only give them back if they could pass the do-it-yourself Breathalyser test that he had created to help them keep death off the road and also to keep their driving licenses.

George had a tape-recorder set up in the corner of the bar, and when customers requested their keys on leaving he would hold the microphone in front of them and say, 'Right, sir, first of all would you please breathe into this and say four times in reasonably quick succession, 'Pleasant Pheasant Plucker'.* Any sign of slurring, and George refused to give them their keys. Those who dissented would have the tape recording played back to them the next day as proof that they were not fit to drive.

It was George's response to the official Breathalyser test introduced by Transport Minister Barbara Castle in 1966, and which at first threatened to wreck his business. The only slight complication he had had so far with anybody taking the 3-Ps test – 'taking the Pees,' as it had become known – came when Bernie Biddle failed it. This meant that his hearse, with an uncomplaining

---

*Please try it aloud, dear reader, and see if you are sober enough to carry on reading: Pleasant Pheasant Plucker... Pleasant Pheasant Plucker... Pleasant Pheasant Plucker.... Pleasant Pheasant Plucker. Thank you.

occupant on board, had to stay in the pub car park overnight. 'Well,' said Bernie, coming to terms with the decision, 'it will be more peaceful there than in our chapel of rest.' Out of respect, customers leaving the pub late that night were asked not to bang their car doors.

Sidney Bliss, the most regular of regulars at the Pleasant Pheasant Plucker, arrived ten minutes early for the date of his dreams. He handed the keys for his 'crumpet catcher', a red 1950s Jaguar XK120, across the bar to George, and then stood watching the door waiting for Sheila Blige to come wiggling in. This, Sidney thought to himself as he ordered his first pint, was going to raise his reputation as a master of the pull by several notches.

Seven o'clock became eight o'clock, and Sidney, supping as slowly as he could, was into his fourth pint, and no sign of Miss Blige. He passed the time putting the world to rights with George and barmaid Nancy Klinger, repeating his complaints about there being too much free love for a man to make a decent living in the dating agency business.

'Well I never give it away,' said Nancy, who was notorious as being anybody's for a gin and tonic and a lift home to her flat all of two hundred yards away. 'I always take my mum's advice, "Protect your penny and one day it will be worth pounds".'

This led the conversation into how the pound had become devalued since the introduction of decimalisation in February 1971. 'Everything has been marked up except sex,' grumbled Sidney. 'While everybody else is rounding their prices up we have had to drop ours, and we're now so desperate that we offer two dates for the price of one.'

Bowler-hatted Ivor Bodie had joined them, which did not please Sidney. He could talk for England, and he was in no mood to have to tune into his deathly Dickensian prose in which he put aitches in where they should not have been and dropped them when they were needed. 'It's the same in my business,' the funeral director said, his face so long that Sidney wondered whether Nancy should give him his drink in a bucket. 'Decimalisation will be the death of the hundertaking game. We could always order our wood to the nearest hinch, but now it's to the nearest centimetre, and it plays 'avoc with our profit margins.'

He extricated his teeth from the whisky glass before continuing. 'Take today, for hinstance,' he said, 'I've hembalmed Mrs Stoneham and prepared Mr Stoneham for hembalming tomorrow.'

Bodie looked at his watch. 'In fact, I might go back and finish the job tonight,' he added. 'Left 'im on the slab. I will bury them together next Friday, Mrs S on top of course. As in life, as in death so to speak. Now hain't that a great ruddy shame that I've got to bury them on top of each other? Before all this metric nonsense, I would 'ave buried them side by side and could 'ave given them room to breathe. But no, we now have to measure the 'oles by metres instead of yards, and it means we're 'aving to dig smaller 'oles. Won't let us dig the wide ones any more. Used to be able to show my clients off under wonderful bloomin' tombstones, works of art they were. But what's the latest bloody order? No 'eadstone above a metre tall. Not a yard, mark you. A bloody metre. Dead liberty it is. You watch, before we know it, they'll be having us order our petrol by the litre instead of by gallons. Don't laugh. You mark my words. The minute Teddy 'eath took us into the Common Market I said, "that's his funeral". Europe? I wouldn't give you tuppence for it. Bloody load of foreigners...'

Sidney left Bodie talking to himself and slipped away to look in the public bar to see if Miss Blige had popped in there. He ordered a pint from Nancy.

'Ivor's still rabbiting away in there,' she said. 'Not a soul listening to him, but it doesn't seem to bother him. S'pose that comes of working with the dead all the time. They can't answer back, can they?'

'We timed him once, and his record for talking without taking a pause is an hour and twenty minutes,' said Sidney. 'And he only shut up then because it was last orders. He's done more talking at the bar than the Lord Chief bloody Justice.'

Sidney suddenly panicked, worrying that Miss Blige might have gone into the saloon bar while he was here talking to Nancy. He drained his glass, and dashed back to the saloon bar.

Bodie was still in full flow. '...and you tell me, 'ave you ever seen a Chinese funeral?' he said to nobody in particular. 'Blowed if I 'ave. That's why there are so many billions of them. And another thing, why don't you see baby pigeons? Are they born fully grown? And why don't you see white dog shit any more? You know, that 'ard white stuff that exploded when you kicked it. What's happened to it all...? I said to my missus the

24

other day, I said as I passed her the shovel, you can't get good gravediggers any more...'

Sidney went and stood alone at the far end of the bar, a now extremely nervous eye on the door. Eight became nine, and a forlorn and three-parts sozzled Sidney was just ordering his ninth pint when the door swung open and in wiggled the fantasy girl. Every head in the bar turned as a searchlight of eyes took in the vision, the men trying to take her clothes off, the women trying to burn her alive.

The good news was that she had arrived. The bad news for Sidney was that she had company.

'Sorry I'm late, Mr Bliss...'

'Shidney, pleashe,' slurred Sidney.

'...Got delayed on a story. This is Ralph, my photographer.'

Sidney shook his hand, while he would have preferred to squeeze his throat. For no justifiable reason, he took an instant dislike to him in the way that a person does when just being parted from logic by a drink too far. Tight blue jeans, hair down to his shoulders, Cuban-heeled boots, and a T-shirt that carried the legend, WOODSTOCK FESTIVAL '69. The only thing missing, thought Sidney, was the make love not war placard. His casual dress was in direct contrast to Sidney's presumed sartorial elegance. Loud made-to-measure Prince of Wales brown check suit, a tight-fitting waistcoat, brogue shoes and a cheesecutter cap. The only thing missing was a bookie's satchel.

'What will you have to drink?' asked Sidney. 'I'm just getting a pint in.'

25

'A rum and coke for me, please,' said Miss Blige.

'I think a large scotch would go down nicely, thanks squire,' said Ralph, smacking his lips.

'Well think again, mush,' said Sidney, meaning it as a joke but, because he was losing control of his tongue, it came out sounding like a sharp put-down.

The photographer put up his hands in surrender. 'Sorry,' he said. 'A single will do.'

Ralph, six feet tall and with the dark brooding looks of a Latino lover, was the right side of thirty. Yes, perhaps there was logic in Sidney's reasoning that this was a man to be despised... or was it envied?

It had taken Sheila Blige just moments to realise that she had arrived too late to get any sense out of a conversation with the dating agency proprietor.

'I didn't expect our date to be a threeshome,' said Sidney, as he handed them their drinks.

'Don't worry about me, squire,' said Ralph. 'I'm just the chauffeur.'

'This is not really my idea of a date, Mr Bliss,' said Miss Blige. 'I would much prefer to speak to you in your office when there are, um...'

She glanced across at Ivor Bodie talking to himself at the bar while he fished the top set of his teeth out of his whisky glass.

'...fewer distractions.'

'Sshcertainly,' said Sidney. 'Quite undershtood. This ish not the placesh for you and I to have a little chat. What shay I run you home, and we can talk in my car on the way? It'sh a Jag. Red, XK120. Twin-cam sixsh-shilinder three point four litre engine. The worksh.'

Before Miss Blige had time to respond, Sidney had waved an arm to attract the landlord. 'George, my car keysh pleashe.'

Drinkwater stood behind the bar with the keys in one hand, and the tape-recorder microphone in the other. 'Right, Sidney', he said. 'You know the rules of the road. First of all would you please breathe into this and say four times in reasonably quick succession, Pleasant Pheasant Plucker.'

'No problem,' Sidney said as he swayed against the bar, giving a crooked grin in the direction of the wide-eyed Sheila Blige. He noticed that she could not take her eyes off him.

George switched on the tape-recorder. 'Peasant Pleashant Pucker,' said Sidney, and then holding up a hand. 'Shorry, I washn't ready. I'll shtart again. 'Pleashant Peashant Plucket. That wash better. Right, start recording now.'

'I already am recording, said George, 'and your test has started. You've got two more goes.'

'Pheshant Pleashant Puck... oh, bugger. Right, this is the one. Get thoshe keysh ready.'

Sidney took a deep breath ready for a real run at it. 'Here we go, right, quiet now... Pleashant Peashant Phucker... oh, fu...'

George now had his back to him as he returned the car keys to a cabinet, and locked it.

Miss Blige and Ralph were preparing to leave.

'I supposhe you'll have to schauffeur the two of ush, Alf.'

'It's Ralph, squire,' the photographer said, walking

Miss Blige to the door. 'And I'm afraid I've only got a 1960s MV Augusta, 350cc motorbike, room for just two. Good night, squire.'

'I really am sorry I was late, Mr Bliss,' said Miss Blige as she wiggled away. 'I'll call in to see you in your office tomorrow morning at eleven o'clock, and we can talk about how I get on your books. Night, night.'

Sidney stood staring blankly at the door swinging shut. To his right Ivor Bodie was going on about how Winston Churchill's spectacular state funeral was his finest hour ('Surely you mean final hour,' said Nancy), and behind him George Drinkwater was shaking his head. 'It beats me,' he said, 'why an absolute corker like that reporter girl should need to join a dating agency. I'd give her one for free.'

Without pausing for breath, Ivor Bodie said, 'Her knockers are too big for my taste.'

One down for Einstein.

Sidney was having trouble focusing on Miss Blige as she sat opposite him in his office with her mini-skirted legs crossed. He was squinting not so much because he was dazzled by the sight of her but because of a black cloud of a hangover. Four more pints followed by a whisky chaser had just about finished him off the previous night, and he had been poured out of a taxi at midnight to find the front door bolted by Rhinobottom. He spent the night sleeping in the garden shed, and was now of little use to man or beast.

Sophie had given him the cold tongue treatment on their way to the office, squashed together in her orange

Mini ('Like a rhino riding a tricycle,' he'd thought when she first drove home in it from the car showroom.) He would pick up his Jaguar from the pub car park later.

He had forgotten about Miss Blige coming at eleven, and was drinking a bubbling glass of Andrews Liver Salts when she pushed open the door and made a stunning entrance. Salt bubbles went up Sidney's nose as she wiggled into view, and he let out a loud burp.

Sophie, sitting in the corner of the office, stood up. 'Good morning, Miss...?

'Blige,' she said. 'Sheila Blige. I did tell Mr Bliss last night that I would be here at eleven.'

'You were with Mr Bliss last night?' said Sophie.

'Yes, at the Pleasant Pheasant Plucker,' she said. 'I was a long time coming I'm afraid, and I think at one stage Mr Bliss must have thought I was not going to come at all.'

'Really,' said Sophie coldly. 'I've found the opposite is usually the case.'

'Miss Blige is here to talk about becoming a client,' said Sidney, trying to repair what was obviously already dangerous ground between Sophie and the reporter.

'In that case,' said Sophie, 'I'll go into the back office and let you get on with it. Perhaps without me distracting you you could come together.'

She sniffed and made a haughty exit.

Sidney put the still-bubbling glass of Andrews into a side draw on his desk. 'Right, Miss Blige...'

'Sheila, please.'

'Right Sheila,' said Sidney, trying to smile through his hangover, 'what can I do you for?'

29

'I am here on an assignment suggested by my editor,' she said, 'and between you and me, Mr Bliss...'

'Sidney, please.'

Behind the slot in the computer, Sophie was almost gagging.

'...between you and me, Sidney, if I mess this up it will be the end of my six months trial run at the *Advertiser*.'

'Oh dear,' said Sidney. 'We can't have that. What can I do to help your career?'

'Well, I would like to become a client on the books of your dating agency.'

'No problem whatsoever, Sheila,' said Sidney, reaching for a filing card. 'Blimey, it will be an honour.'

'Just one thing,' said Sheila. 'I want your permission to be able to write about my experiences.'

'Uh, write about them? You mean keep a diary? Well that's up to you...'

'No, I mean for the newspaper.'

'For the *Advertiser*?'

Sheila forced a laugh. 'Well not for the *News of the World*.'

Sophie forced herself not to be sick.

'Blimey, we wouldn't want the News of the Screws trying to expose us,' said Sidney. 'Not that I've got a lot to expose. But what sort of thing would you write about?'

'Well, let me be honest with you, Sidney,' Sheila said, leaning forward to give him a full view of her cleavage in what was a low-cut sweater that nearly met the hem of her micro-mini skirt. 'My editor is very, very cynical about the whole business of dating agencies. In fact he went so far as to call them a big con.'

''as your editor ever had a bunch of fives in his mush?' Sidney said instinctively, reverting to the days when he was a professional middleweight boxer. 'What d'you take me for? Do I look the sort of geezer who would try to make capital out of the loneliness and heartache of loveless people?'

Sitting there in his crumpled Prince of Wales check suit and with an already heavily lined face further creased from lack of sleep, Sidney did not look the epitome of trustworthiness. But Sheila Blige was obliged to be accommodating for the sake of her story.

'Of course not,' she said. 'And that's why I want to write a story that puts the record straight. What I would like is to join your dating agency as a lonely heart, incognito of course. We can make up a name and a background for me, and then I will write about my experiences in the paper. Of course, I will not use the proper names of the people I get to meet. So what is there to lose?'

She fluttered her eyelashes at Sidney, who wanted to do likewise but the hangover was pressing his eyelids almost shut. He made do with a smile that was more grimace because of the hammer in his head.

'Can you excuse me a moment, please Sheila,' he said. 'I just need to have a quick board meeting about this.'

He went into the back office where Sophie was stalking the room like an enraged rhino.

'The answer is no,' she said before Sidney had even

31

opened her mouth.

'I haven't said anything yet,' protested Sidney.

'Well save your breath, and just go out there and tell that tabloid tart that it's just not on.'

'But this could be just the break we want.'

'The only break you get will be a broken neck when I push you and her down the stairs,' Sophie fumed.

'But listen, lollipop,' Sidney said, calling into the caverns of his memory for terms of endearment. 'This will be unbelievable publicity. We couldn't buy it. It's just what we need to get the business up and running again.'

'You are honestly not naive enough to think that that eyelash-fluttering, thigh-flashing, bum-wobbling little trollop is going to write anything but a sleazy exposé, do you?'

'Ah, so now we have it,' said Sidney, making his eyes blaze beyond the cloud of the hangover. 'It's because she's a beautiful-looking bit of stuff that you are so anti it. If it had been a dark and handsome male reporter, you would have been singing a different tune.'

Sophie stamped her foot, and two floors down below Mr Stoneham fell off the embalming table.

'It's nothing to do with what she looks like,' she said. 'But it is all to do with her motives and what she'll write. What guarantee have you got that she won't go to the *News of the World* and expose us for the corrupt business partners that we are? The last time we sent any couple out on a genuine date was when England won the World Cup in 1966 and we paired my hairdresser Gladys Partridge with a Jimmy Greaves look-alike. She

32

only went out with him because she felt sorry for him after Alf Ramsey had left Greaves out of the team for the Final at Wembley.'

'But that was more than five years ago.'

'Exactly, and ever since we've been ducking and diving more than Ronnie Biggs. You've even sent your own mother out on dates, and just last week you hit a new low when you sent me to meet that vicar from Darlington. It's the first time anybody has groped me while making the sign of the cross.'

Sidney took a letter from his jacket pocket. 'This came in the post this morning,' he said. 'It's from the bank. They've given us fourteen days to clear our twenty thousand pounds overdraft or they're going to recommend us for bankruptcy. Nice of 'em, ain't it. I never write to them and complain when they've got all my money in their bank.'

'The last time we were in the black King George VI's picture was on the pound notes.'

'But if I *did* have money in the bank, I wouldn't be writing them rude letters, that's all I'm saying. Anyway, if we don't start getting business soon we are done for. We might as well go downstairs to Ivor Bodie and ask him to bury us, me on top.'

'So what are we going to do?'

'There's only one thing for it,' said Sidney. 'We've got to take the gamble on Sheila Blige writing an article that will get the punters flocking through our door.'

'And did Sheila Blige?'

'Did Sheila Blige what?'

'Oblige?'

'Don't talk rubbish, woman. All I had was one drink with her in the pub last night.'

'And it was just one drink that made you paralytic?'

'That's right. Just one drink – the ninth one as I remember.'

'Oh all right, then. Let the pouting pen pusher free to do her worst. But I'm warning you, Sidney Bliss, if she lets us down and ruins our business you and I will have a proper date. In the divorce court.'

In the front office, the pouting pen pusher was smiling happily to herself. Here cometh an exposé.

That afternoon Sidney put a small-ad in the *Advertiser* that he and Miss Blige concocted together:

PALE NURSE SEEKS MAN TO BRING SUNSHINE TO A DARK LIFE. HOBBIES: NUDE SUNBATHING, NIGHTCLUBBING AND GROWING BIG, BIG BANANAS. ARE YOU MAN ENOUGH FOR ME? BOX 5609.

If that doesn't pull 'em in, said Sidney to himself, nothing will. The man serving behind the fish and chip shop counter looked at the advertisement that Sidney handed to him. 'Very nice, Mr Bliss,' he said, 'but I think you mean this for the small-ads department next door.'

As Sidney walked out of the chippie, the fryer shouted: 'Put me down for next Wednesday.'

34

3

BERNIE BIDDLE slipped out of the chapel of rest while Mr Bodie was telling the latest reluctant occupant about the scandal of rising wood prices, and with giant strides he cleared the stairs to the Wedded Bliss Matrimonial Dating Agency three at a time. He was being propelled by impatience and frustration at not having had a single date since signing on and parting with his ten pounds deposit.

As he approached the outer office like a gathering storm Sidney was sitting with his feet up on the desk thinking of money-raising schemes. Sophie was in the back office secretly typing out the second chapter of her first novel, *Ten Ways to Murder Your Husband*. Chapter One had dealt with death by strangulation, and she was now cooking up ways to poison the husband in the book, a fictitious character who wore loud check suits, drove a Jaguar sports car and was a boozer and womaniser. She had called him Rodney but for some unfathomable reason kept making typing errors so that he continually appeared as Sidney.

Bernie's sudden entrance rudely interrupted Sidney's daydream about the number of clients the advertisement for Sheila Blige would pull. At least two thousand he reckoned, and at an enrolment fee of ten pounds a time that was the bank overdraft cleared in one hit. They had decided they would call her Eileen Overr to protect her true identity, and to give just a little hint of promiscuity. The daydream was broken by the door swinging almost off its hinges as the heavy-handed, leaden-footed, huge-framed Bernie Biddle clumped into the office. A sugar plum fairy he was not. It had been said behind his back in the Pleasant Pheasant Plucker that his hulking appearance in the Chapel of Rest frightened the corpses to life but that Bodie quickly bored them back to death. It was born-clumsy Bernie who had once managed to knock the coffin off its pedestal just before the start of a funeral service in the local church. Bodie's cheap wood had shattered, and they had to prop up the corpse, a local greengrocer in his seventies, in the choir stall. The vicar started his address to the congregation by saying, 'We are gathered here to pay our final respects to Harry Hawkeswell, who we are delighted to have with us today in the tenor section of the choir.' It was later claimed that he had been the only one singing in tune.

'We normally see clients by appointment only,' said Sidney, as Bernie's giant shadow fell over him, 'but as it's you and we know you I'll try to give you ten minutes from my busy schedule. This, of course, is on the understanding that we have to bill you a fiver for consultancy time.'

Bernie sat down facing Sidney across his desk. 'But I've already given you a tenner, Mr Bliss,' he moaned, 'and I've not so much as 'ad a sniff. I know I'm not God's gift, but surely you can find somebody to go out with me. If not, can I have my tenner back? It was you after all, Mr Bliss, who said "no layee, no payee".'

Sidney decided on the friendly approach to dampen

down the familiar flames of anger and frustration that he was accustomed to seeing in clients unreasonably expecting more for their money.

'Why do you persist on calling me Mr Bliss when we've known each other more than twenty years?' he said, leaning across the desk behind his warmest smile. 'It's Sidney, please.'

'It's at Mr Bodie's insistence, Mr Bliss,' said Bernie. 'He says I have to be formal with everybody because you never know when you're going to have to embalm 'em, box 'em, bear 'em, bury 'em, or burn 'em. It's what Mr Bodie calls the five Bs of the burial business. He says at all times be courteous but distant as whoever you're with is a potential client. Mr Bodie says familiarity breeds conscience. If you get too familiar with somebody, he says, you find it hard to bury 'em. I even call my dad Mr Biddle.'

'I understand,' said Sidney, running a finger round the inside of his collar as he reacted with discomfort at the fleeting thought of being left in the hands of Bodie and Co at the end of his days. 'Now then, Bernie, what appears to be the problem?'

'Like I say, I've not 'ad a sniff yet,' he said. 'When you talked me into joining the agency that night at the 3Ps, you guaranteed that I would 'ave at least half a dozen dates in the first week. I've not so much as 'ad a touch of a woman's 'and in mine, unless you count Mrs Stoneham when I was doing the embalming.'

'Bernie, Bernie, Bernie,' said Sidney, 'don't you realise the standards we set 'ere in the Wedded Bliss Agency? While you're busily embalming and waxing with loving

37

care downstairs, we are being just as particular and with an equal penchant for perfectionism up 'ere. Now tell me if I'm right, Bernie – when you're working on one of your clients don't you do your best to get a smile on their face?'

'Oh yes, Mr Bodie insists on it. He says that he doesn't want anybody looking dissatisfied when they leave us. He always says to our clients while they're lying there, "A smile makes your life worthwhile".'

'Exactly, Bernie. And that's our philosophy as well. It's our aim to bring a smile to your face by finding you the best possible date mate. We want only the best for our clients, and so we wait until the computer makes the perfect match before we bring you together in a ferment of anticipation, expectation and...'

'Lust?' suggested Bernie.

'Uh, well, all right, for the want of a better word,' said Sidney, while in the back office Sophie typed the sentence, 'It was his lusting after women that had made her determined to do away with ~~Sidney~~ Rodney...'

'I'll tell you what I'll do,' said Sidney. 'As you've taken the trouble to come and see us, I'll take your fiver consultancy fee and then bring Mrs Bliss in to bring your card up to date and run it through the computer. I have a feeling that this could be your lucky day. Meanwhile, you'll have to excuse me while I make a call in the back office.'

He held out his hand, and Bernie went to shake it, 'No,' said Sidney. 'I was hoping you'd cross my palm with a crisp fiver.'

'Oh, yeah, of course Mr Bliss,' Bernie said, reaching

into his wallet and bringing out five one pound notes that were transferred to Sidney's inside pocket with the same blinding speed that he could produce a calling card.

He then went into the back room where Sophie was typing the sentence, 'She sprinkled the arsenic into ~~Sidney's~~ Rodney's porridge and stirred it.'

'Right, Sophie,' he said. 'Computer duty.'

She was so startled by his sudden appearance in the room that her fingers slipped on the keyboard. 'God, Rodney, you made me jump,' she said. 'Your porridge is nearly ready.'

'Who the bleedin' hell's Rodney?' Sidney said. 'And I don't want porridge for me lunch, thank you very much.'

'Did I say Rodney? Silly me. I was getting you mixed up with my husband.'

'But I *am* your husband.'

'Of course you are. How could I forget?'

'Just get out there and keep Bernie Biddle amused with the computer show, while I make out a card for him. I'll fix him up with Phoebe Scratchitt.'

'You rotter,' she said. 'What's Phoebe done to deserve him?'

'Shouldn't you be saying what's Bernie done to deserve Phoebe? In fact they deserve each other. Go on, turn the computer on.'

While Sophie joined Bernie in the front office, Sidney looked up the file card on Phoebe Scratchitt. She was twenty-seven going on forty, and had been on the agency books from when the business first started eight years earlier. In that time she had been matched with one hundred and twenty-seven clients and had failed to get to second base with any of them. Her pebble-lensed glasses had been something of a handicap, but these had now been replaced by contact lenses. The trouble was she was extremely short-sighted in one eye and very long-sighted in the other, and she kept putting the lenses in the wrong eyes, which gave her an odd and distorted perspective on life. Agency dating partners taking her out to eat found it fairly off-putting when she would hold the menu up within half an inch of her eye to read it, and then hold the wine glass at arm's length before finding the route to her mouth. But she had a heart of gold, as the fourteen stray cats that she kept at her one bedroomed apartment would testify. Phoebe had reached such a desperation stage that she kept having her name altered in the agency file in the hope that a new, more appealing sounding identity would change her luck. At the moment she was down as Monica Crackitt.

Sophie pushed the switch that started the 'Date Data Computer' whirring, the gramophone turntables spinning and the lightbulbs from a 1968 Christmas tree flashing on and off. Bernie watched with wide-eyed fascination. 'This is all too scientific for me to understand, Mrs Bliss' he said. 'It's great. It's just like watching a Christmas tree light up.'

'Quite,' said Sophie, placing his card in the right hand entry slot. Sidney, standing on the other side, took it and placed it in the typewriter. He typed the codeword, PEBBLE.

'What 'appens now?' said Bernie on the other side of the wall.

'Well, the card is going through the sophisticated and expertly programmed computer system,' explained Sophie, with her fingers crossed. 'It is searching for any matching hobbies, likes, dislikes and mutual interests. It will shortly come out at the data exit point with, hopefully, a codeword, which will mean it has found what it considers a possible ideal date mate.'

'Cor, I can 'ardly wait. It's amazin' what they can do today. Mr Bodie says that one day people will sit with computers on their laps. But your computer would be too 'eavy, wouldn't it, Mrs Bliss?'

'For somebody who deals in death, Mr Bodie appears to be quite a visionary,' said Sophie, making conversation while waiting for Sidney to feed the card through the exit channel. They liked to wait five minutes to give the client the feeling the computer was giving them a good search for their money.

'Oh, he is, Mrs Bliss,' said Bernie. 'He says that one day in the not too distant future we will be able to feed paper through the telephone on what he calls a fix machine. Newspapers, he says, will cost six shillings, bread will cost ten shillings a loaf, there will be pound coins instead of pound notes, and this will make you laugh, he says that beer will cost nearly two pounds a pint. Nobody will get drunk then, that's for sure. That's a day's wages for me. Mr Bodie also says that our Parliament will be based somewhere in Europe and that you will reach it by going under the Channel in a train. Between you and me, Mrs Bliss, I think Mr Bodie sometimes lets his imagination run away with him. I mean to say, our Parliament somewhere in Europe!'

'Quite, Mr Biddle,' Sophie said, silently thinking that Bodie was quite mad. 'We will stay as proudly and reliably British as good old roast beef.'

Sidney pressed the buzzer in the back office to signal that he was ready to push the card through. Sophie collected it, and turned off the computer.

'What does it say?' said Bernie with the excitement of a boy waiting for his Christmas present to be opened. ''as she got big knockers?'

Sophie read the PEBBLE codeword for Monica Crackitt, alias Phoebe Scratchitt. 'I'll just cross-check it,' she said, pulling open the filing cabinet that was jammed solid with files, of which ninety-five per cent were out of date. She was looking for Phoebe's file when Mr Mischief came tapping metaphorically on her shoulder, and almost by accident she pulled out the new file that Sidney had code named WIGGLE.

'Here it is,' said Sophie, lowering her voice just above a whisper in case Sidney's ears were flapping. 'Her name is Miss Eileen Overr. She's in her mid-twenties, likes sunbathing, club outings and eating exotic fruit.'

'What sort of club outings?'

Sophie pretended to study the card for the answer. 'Nature clubs, it seems.'

'We've got a lot in common then,' said Bernie. 'I like nature. I've been to see *Bambi* three times.'

'Well the two of you should get along,' said Sophie. 'Where and when would you like to meet her?'

'I want it to be tonight, but I don't finish until nine-

42

thirty. Tell her I'll meet her at a quarter to ten in the Pleashant Pheashant Pucker,' said Bernie, his excitement so great that he was already failing the car-key test.

'I don't think that's advisable,' said Sophie, knowing the odds were that Sidney would be in the bar. 'She's the type who likes to be wined and dined in a nice restaurant.'

'Good, so do I. Tell her that I'll meet her in the high street Wimpy Bar at a quarter to ten.'

'All right, Mr Biddle. I shall telephone her this afternoon and will come down to see you if there are any problems. Your agency codeword when you meet her is "destiny".'

'How will I know her?'

'She's got big knockers,' said Sophie, unable to think of any more fitting description for somebody who was already featuring in her novel as 'the girl with the giggle and the wiggle from hell'.

Bernie went back to his work whistling, and he put the biggest smile on Mrs Stoneham that her face had ever worn.

Eileen Overr, alias Sheila Blige, felt strangely nervous as she wiggled towards the Wimpy Bar. Even though this was not for real, she felt a sense of excitement tinged with apprehension at the prospect of meeting somebody on a blind date. One day, she thought, she would suggest it as a format for a television game show with that young singer Cilla Black co-hosting it with the man of her dreams, Cliff Richard.

She felt happy in the knowledge that Ralph was not

going to be too far away, armed with a hidden camera with which he would snatch pictures of her together with her 'date mate'. Mrs Bliss, who she found as cold as a fishmonger's fingers, had told her little about the man she was about to meet other than his name was Bernie and that he would approach her with the codeword 'destiny'.

'Why can't you tell me anything about him?' she asked on the telephone.

'Because,' said Sophie, 'it's agency policy just to give the introduction. It is important you get to know all about each other by searching for common ground through conversation. If you go in to it knowing too much about each other you stifle the relationship before it has started by having a preconceived view based on a few facts and figures. We have an agency saying, "talk, walk and hawk".'

'Hawk?' said Sheila, making notes as a foundation for her article.

'That's right,' said Sophie. 'Watch your partner like a hawk while you walk and talk. Find out from each other's mannerisms and body language whether you have enough in common to take the relationship a stage further.'

As Sheila approached the Wimpy Bar she was surprised to see a hearse draw up outside, and she wondered if somebody had died. Ever since she was a little girl she had always got a strange tingle when she saw a hearse, and was never able to understand why. Tonight, for some reason, the tingle went down her back like a tropical breeze, and she gave an involuntary shudder. It was a nice feeling.

The driver of the hearse, a giant of a man dressed all in black except for a red cravat, got out and as he stepped on to the pavement he tripped up the kerb. He went hurtling head first towards the Wimpy Bar door, which was opened by a customer just about to leave. The stumbling man fell inside the door like a huge sack of coal being delivered, causing screams of fright and then shrieks of laughter from the customers inside.

Sheila followed him in, and managed to stifle her own scream when he picked himself up and said to her, 'Dysentery, Miss?'

'I beg your pardon?'

'Dysentery. The agency codeword, Miss.'

Sheila searched for her voice which had temporarily deserted her along with most of her senses. 'Uh, do you mean destiny?'

'That's the word,' Bernie said, holding out a hand. 'I'm Bernie Biddle, Miss Leanover. Lovely to meet yer.'

As he led her to a table in the far corner of the Wimpy Bar, Sheila tried desperately to think of an escape plan but she was trapped, at least until she could find an excuse to leave the restaurant.

They sat facing each other across a table for four, but Bernie was so big that he filled the two seats opposite her.

'D'you come here often?' he asked.

'Uh, only sometimes,' she said.

'Like when you're hungry.'

'Uh, yes. That's it.'

'Have you been with the agency long?'

45

'Joined yesterday,' she said.

'Oh. So I'm your first date.'

'That's right.'

'Lucky me. Hope it's going to be your last... uh, meaning, Miss Leanover,' Bernie said, stuttering and blushing, 'meaning, that is, that I hope you won't want to see any others.'

'It's Overr,' said Sheila.

'But we've only just met,' said Bernie. 'What 'ave I done wrong?'

'No, it's Overr. Eileen Overr, with two Rs... because I like to roll my Rs.'

'Yes, I had noticed,' said Bernie, his blush becoming a fire. ''ere, Miss Overr, you're not going to believe it but you're a dead ringer for a girl what works in the newspaper office next door to me. But she's not as good looking as what you are.'

'Thank you,' said Sheila, trying hard to copy Bernie's blush.

Two tables away Ralph was snapping busily with a miniature camera hidden in a shoebox with a hole cut for the lens to poke through. He had his left hand clicking away inside the box, while on the table was a false hand and arm that had been inserted into the sleeve of his coat.

Bernie handed Sheila a menu. 'What you going to have, Miss Overr?'

'Call me Eileen,' Sheila said.

'Sorry, but I have to be formal.'

'Because it's our first date?'

'No, because Mr Bodie says so.'

46

'Mr Bodie?'

'My boss. He says that you could be my next client.'

'Your next client? What do you do for a living, Bernie?'

'I'm an undertaker's assistant.'

Sheila felt herself go pale under her liberally applied Max Factor make-up. 'That explains the hearse,' she said. 'Do you, um, always drive around in it?'

'No, only when I'm driving it. I usually go by bike.'

She was driven by a sudden impulse. 'Bernie,' she said, leaning forward and whispering, 'I don't know how to ask you this, but would you mind giving me a ride in the hearse?'

'It'll be my pleasure, Miss, as soon as we've had our Wimpy and chips.'

'I don't want to wait to eat,' said Sheila, not knowing what had come over her. 'I want to go in the hearse. Now.'

'Anything you say, Miss. This will make it a first date for us both to remember.'

'You bet,' said Sheila, dragging him by the hand and out of the Wimpy, with Ralph chasing after them with a shoebox in one hand and a cheeseburger in the other. The door of the Wimpy Bar swung in his face, catching his false hand and dragging it out of his coat sleeve and on to the floor. A girl leaving behind him fainted into her boyfriend's arms.

'Must be pregnant,' said the waitress to the chef.

'Where would you like me to take you?' asked Bernie, sitting straight and proud behind the wheel of his beloved hearse.

'To the cemetery, of course.' Sheila said, astonished at the excitement she was feeling. Here she was sitting next to a giant oaf in a hearse of all things, and she was boiling over with what she could only describe as an overwhelming sexual yearning. Ex-boyfriends had always complained that she was frigid, but since climbing into the hearse she felt as if she was on fire.

'But the cemetery will be closed,' Bernie said.

'You'll get us in,' Sheila said. 'I know you will. Tell them you're the night shift.'

'Yes, Miss,' he said, putting his foot down and heading for the cemetery.

Sheila looked at the coffin in the back. 'Who's back there?' she asked, breathing heavily.

'Mr Stoneham,' said Bernie. 'Mr Bodie said it was causing a bad atmosphere in the Chapel of Rest having both Mr and Mrs Stoneham in there, so he told me to take him out for an evening drive.'

The lights from oncoming cars picked up the glint of excitement shining in Sheila's eyes. Behind them an MV Augusta 350cc motorbike was struggling to keep up.

Cedric, the cemetery night watchman, was woken by the ringing of the gate bell.

'What the bleedin' 'ell do you want at this time of night?' he said, recognising the hulking outline of Bernie. 'Don't you know it's gorn eleven o'clock. Everybody's asleep in 'ere.'

'Just let me in for 'alf an 'our, Cedric,' said Bernie. 'I'll make it worth your while. I dropped something by one of the graves this morning, and I want to pick it up before somebody else nicks it.'

48

He slipped Cedric a pound note, and he reluctantly opened the gates and let the hearse through.

Two minutes later he accepted another pound note, this time to let an MV Augusta through with a bloke who said he wanted to visit the grave of his old mother. 'Blimey,' he said, 'you'll 'ave to push that thing around, otherwise you'll make enough noise to wake her.'

Bernie drove deep into the cemetery before Sheila ordered him to stop.

'Right,' she said, her face flushed with passion and anticipation, 'let's get into the back and have it off.'

In his excitement, Bernie moved too quickly to climb over his seat, forgot to duck and banged his head against the roof of the hearse. As he fell into the back his head crashed against the coffin so hard that the lid shifted, and Bernie went out like a light. 'Thanks for getting it off,' said Sheila.

When he came around some five minutes later Bernie could not believe what he was seeing. There was Miss Leanover *inside* the coffin with Mr Stoneham, and she was moaning and groaning and cuddling up to him.

'Get out of there you crazy woman,' said Bernie, suddenly going off his date mate.

From behind a gravestone ten yards away, a miniature camera with a new Japanese magic eye that could see in the dark was filling a roll of film.

Three minutes later Cedric could not believe his eyes or ears as the hearse, with Bernie Biddle at the wheel, came roaring up to the gates. He managed to get them open just before he crashed through them. Cedric had just closed the gates when an MV Augusta going like the clappers collided with them, the driver pitching over the handlebars and face first into the gravel driveway. Cedric dashed off and called an ambulance when he saw that the motorcyclist's left hand had been torn off in the crash.

It was an hour later when Bernie, with the aid of a trolley, returned the coffin to the Chapel of Rest. He had thrown Miss Leanover out at the high street bus stop, and told her that he never wanted to clap eyes on her again. She had mumbled something about reading it all in the *Advertiser* but he knew that nobody had seen them to report it.

As he put the coffin down, he noticed that Mr Stoneham was now wearing an even bigger smile than Mrs Stoneham. It was the happiest day of his life.

4

THE MORNING after the nurse small-ad appeared in the *Advertiser* Sidney got a strange telephone call at home from Ivor Bodie. 'I want you here at the office straight away,' he said, his teeth clicking in time like a snare drum accompaniment. 'You're holding up my funeral.' That was it. Then the telephone was slammed down. It was the shortest speech that Bodie had made in his life.

Sidney reported to Rhinobottom that he was going in ahead of her, and Sophie revealed that she was taking the day off to finish her third chapter. This was called Murder by Contract, and she wanted to give uninterrupted thinking time to just how to put out a contract on a husband. What, she wondered, would the price be on the head of somebody like Sidney. Oops! She mentally crossed out that thought, and substituted Rodney.

A hearse and two mourners' cars were parked outside the Bodie and Co funeral home. Sidney drove his Jaguar up behind them, and then joined an obviously agitated Ivor Bodie who was standing on the pavement marking time with fidgety feet. 'And about time,' was the greeting Sidney got. ''ow am I supposed to be able to conduct my business with this lot blocking the way to the Chapel of Rest?'

He indicated two huge sacks of mail that had been dumped in the doorway of the funeral home like a

51

couple of body bags.

Sidney took a closer look, and his eyes lit up when he realised they were both addressed to the Wedded Bliss Agency.

'This is not good enough,' fumed the funeral director, his black-beribboned top hat shaking as it rested on his ears. 'How am I supposed to get Mr and Mrs Stoneham over this obstacle course? We're taking them on their final journey, not entering them in the Grand flipping National.'

'Sorry,' Sidney said. 'But you could have moved them to one side.'

'Hoh no,' said Bodie. 'I've learned my lesson. Last time I touched something that was hobstructing me in my work, it was a dustcart by the way, the unions called a strike and the council workers at the cemetery refused to bury my client. Just 'cos I released the 'andbrake and pushed the cart out of the way. 'ow was I to know it was on an incline and that at the bottom of the 'ill was a duck pond? And 'ow was I to know that the foreman was 'aving a kip in the front passenger seat? Hoh no, Mr Biddle, you move your own mailbags.'

Sidney almost gave himself a hernia carrying the two mailbags, one at a time, up the four flights of stairs to his office. He was driven on by adrenalin pumped to maximum levels at the thought of his overdraft being cleared by just one small-ad insert. What would the response be if he kept it running for a month?

He was just getting his breath back and preparing to open the first mailbag when there was a sharp rat-tat on his office door. 'Enter!' he shouted. 'It's open. You don't 'ave to make a bleedin' date to turn the doorknob.'

The door swung open and in walked two dark-suited men carrying black briefcases and wearing mournful looks. 'You've wasted your energy coming up here,' said Sidney. 'The funeral's leaving from downstairs.'

'Mr Bliss?' said one.

'Mr Sidney Bliss?' said the other.

Sidney had a feeling he had not experienced since the day his collar was felt by a detective who wanted to question him over a false claim of harassment made by one of his clients, who had mistaken his trying to help her on with her coat as a quick, uninvited grope.

'Uh, depends on who's asking?' he said through a suddenly constricted throat.

'Are you Sidney Bliss?' said one.

'Sidney Bertram Bliss?' said the other.

'Yes, I am one and the same,' Sidney admitted, realising they knew exactly who he was.

'We're from Her Majesty's Inland Revenue,' said one.

'The Fraud investigation branch,' said the other.

'Well you don't want me, pal,' said Sidney, hoping his face was not mirroring the sudden sickness that was hitting the pit of his stomach. 'You'll be wasting your time talking to me about fraid, I'm afraud.'

'We would like you to answer just a few questions.' said one.

'Purely voluntarily, of course,' said the other.

'And what if I refuse?' Sidney asked, trying to put up a camouflage of hostility while inside he was all of a jelly.

'Well if you don't co-operate...' said one.

'...we will come down on you that much harder for wasting our time and not co-operating when we launch an official investigation of your affairs,' said the other.

'So we recommend very strongly...' said one.

'...that you help us now, and it will save a lot of time and aggravation at a later date,' said the other.

Sidney capitulated. 'Take a seat,' he said, pushing the two sacks of mail into a corner of the office and then sitting opposite them behind his desk.

'Don't suppose I could interest either of you in a date while you're here, can I?' he said, forcing a chuckle. Neither One nor Two moved a face muscle.

Sidney studied his two uninvited visitors. One was short, about five foot seven, but was made to look shorter by his six foot three inch tall companion who had a sallow, almost yellow complexion that suggested he had just had Ivor Bodie's final waxing treatment. The short one talked in a strong Geordie accent, while the other had a Brummie voice that came from his boots and it seemed as if every sentence needed a kick start.

'We were led to understand from our last correspondence with you, Mr Bliss...' said one.

'...that your business was so bad that you could not even afford the price of a postage stamp, and there was not one on your envelope,' said the other.

'...but looking around,' said one, looking around at the two bulging mailbags.

'...it would seem business is flourishing,' said the other.

'You just happen to have come on a good day,'

Sidney said, one of the few statements he knew he could make quite honestly and openly.

'A very good day...' said one, looking again at the mailbags.

'...very good indeed,' said the other.

'Look, gentlemen, I know you've got a job to do,' said Sidney in a cards-on-the-table tone of voice. 'And so 'ave I. Let's help each other by getting this interview over and done with as soon as possible. I've got nothing to hide, so fire away with your questions.'

'That suits...'

'...us just fine.'

'In your last tax return, Mr Bliss, you claimed...'

'...that your income was two thousand four hundred and twenty three pounds...'

'...five shillings and sixpence, in old money...'

'While your expenditure, you claimed, was...'

'...four thousand, one hundred and two pounds...'

'...seven shillings and twopence, in old money.'

'Correct,' said Sidney, trying hard to follow two minds with but a single thought.

'So how was it that you were able to afford...' said one.

'...to run a Jaguar motorcar, have a two-week holiday in the South of France...' said the other.

'...and buy a diamond bracelet that, according to the receipt in our possession, cost the little matter of seven hundred and fifty-eight pounds...'

'...nineteen shillings and sixpence. Just how do you explain this, Mr Bliss?'

One and Two were quiet, waiting for Sidney's

response. Sidney, too, was quiet, waiting for a response to come into his head.

'Can I offer you gentlemen a drink?' he said, reaching into his bottom desk drawer and bringing out a glass. It contained flat Andrews liver salts.

'Just kindly answer...'

'...the questions, Mr Bliss.'

'Well, that's easy,' Sidney said, drinking the Andrews to try to moisten a throat suddenly as dry as an Arab's saddle.

'Let's take them...'

'...in order then. First, the Jaguar car.'

'Well, I need that for appearances sake. It's very important for a man in the sort of line that I am in to look dashing and successful to win the confidence and trust of my clients. I mean, you're not going to put your love life in the 'ands of a geezer who rides around on a bicycle and wears tatty old clothes. That's why I wear this smart clobber and drive an eye-catching car.'

'Yes, Mr Bliss, but what we're interested in...'

'...is how do you pay for them? The clothes and the car.'

'Well I've got the car on the book.'

'HP?'

'Very happy thank you,' said Sidney, hoping to crack their masked faces with what he considered his own brand of razor-sharp humour.

'Do you pay monthly...'

'...or weekly?'

'Very weakly,' said Sidney, borrowing a line from a Morecambe and Wise sketch he had watched on television that weekend.

'This frivolous attitude, Mr Bliss...'

'...is doing you no favours. What about the holiday in the South of France? All we can afford...'

'...is a week in Clacton...'

'...if we're lucky.'

'Well it was a working holiday,' said Sidney. 'I spent nearly all my time down there interviewing prospective clients, telling them about my dating agency and giving them my calling card. It was more business than holiday. Worked myself silly chatting up the birds, I did.'

'Yes, but how did you...'

'...pay for it?'

'As I recall I pawned an, uh, diamond bracelet.'

'And this diamond bracelet...'

'...where did you get the cash to pay for it?'

'Uh, I won it in a game of cards.'

'Poker?'

'No, she wouldn't let me,' said Sidney, firing another blank.

'Where was this game of cards?'

'Um, it was in the back of a hearse.'

'A hearse...?

'...You're not taking a dead liberty with us, are you Mr Bliss?'

'No. It really was. A friend of mine drives a hearse, and this particular day, or night it was, he had no occupant in the back, so to speak, and so we used it for a game of brag.'

'You can name the person...'

'...that you won the money from?'

'Oh yes,' said Sidney, praying for divine help.

'And...'

'...who is it?'

'Uh, his name is Charlie Stoneham. He owns the jeweller's across the road, and after I had won the money from him he sold me the bracelet with a generous discount.'

'We shall be checking that out...'

'...with Mr Stoneham.'

'Fine,' said Sidney. 'That's okay by me. I know he will support me. A good man, Charlie. And his wife saw the transaction. You can check with her, too.'

'And this diamond bracelet...'

'It was for your partner?'

'My partner?'

'In your last tax return you put your business partner down...'

'...as being your wife.'

'Ah, oh yes, my wife. The queen of my soul. Sophie.'

'The diamond bracelet...'

'...was for her?'

'Well, no, not exactly and I would appreciate strictest confidence in this matter, gentlemen. After all, we are all men of the world...'

'Yes, Mr Bliss...'

'...but which world?'

'Well you see, one of my clients was having a hard time, and I bought her the bracelet to help her impress somebody she was meeting on a date that we had arranged for her here at the agency. Now I wouldn't

58

have wanted to bother my wife with a piffling little matter like that.'

'But you then went...'

'...and pawned the bracelet.'

'Ah, yes, well, you see, the client, uh, refused to accept the bracelet. It was all a silly misunderstanding. She seemed to think I was trying to, uh, sort of, uh, get a little favour from her.'

For the next two hours, the tax men grilled Sidney about every bill, receipt and every transaction he had been involved in over the previous three years. At last the third degree was over.

'Well, thank you for your time and co-operation, Mr Bliss,' said one.

'We shall make a full report to our superiors,' said the other.

'Then we shall arrange a second meeting...'

'...when we recommend that you have your accountant...'

'...and a solicitor present to represent you.'

Sidney shook their hands at the door, smiling a forced smile like a footballer who has just been tackled by Norman Hunter but does not want to show that he has been hurt.

He pointed them down the stairs, quietly hoping they would have the same fate as Mr Stoneham.

He had just returned to the unopened mailbags when there was a quiet rapping at the door, and this time it swung open without him having to call out.

Number two taxman, the tall one who looked as if he should have been haunting houses, came in looking furtively around.

'There's nobody in the back office is there?' he said.

'No, I'm on my own,' said Sidney.

'Good, I've told my colleague I've just popped back to pick up some papers that I left on your desk.'

'Where are they?' said Sidney. 'I can't see any.'

'No, I just wanted a quick, quiet word,' he said in barely a whisper.

'What about?' said Sidney, bracing himself for another of his cash-deal skeletons to be rattled.

'That nurse advertisement in yesterday's *Advertiser*,' he said. 'If you can put me right at the top of the date mate list, I could, uh, make a much more favourable report on you.'

'Have you sent in a letter?' asked Sidney, trying to disguise his surprise.

'Ten, actually,' said the tax man. 'Just do your best to let me have first date. That's all, Mr Bliss.'

With that he was out of the door, leaving a cold draught behind him in his wake. 'That's just amazing,' thought Sidney. 'A human tax inspector! He obviously likes big knockers.'

It took Sidney three hours, with a break for a cheese sandwich and a cup of tea, to take out and neatly pile the three thousand envelopes that were stuffed into the mailbags. This was the greatest response the agency had had to any advertisement, in fact an increase of two thousand eight hundred on their previous best reply figure.

Every single letter, with the exception of just one, was

addressed to box 5609 and the Sheila Blige/Eileen Overr ad. There was a lone letter responding to the previous advertisement put in on behalf of Bernie Biddle aimed at buxom barmaids. The letter was signed 'Nancy "Big Knockers" Klinger.'

His feet up on the desk and his mind dancing with thoughts of a minimum thirty thousand pounds in enrolment fees, Sidney started to read through the 'nurse' letters. The first one was so kinky that it almost turned his stomach. The sender had included a photograph of himself, dressed all in black leather and holding what looked like a metal-studded whip. He threw it straight into the wastepaper basket. The next six letters took a similar route, and Sidney realised the wording of the advertisement had been too strong and had attracted every weirdo in the *Advertiser* circulation area.

He at last got into a run of acceptable letters, in which the writers talked about nude sunbathing, clubbing in London's Soho, and banana growing. Nothing wrong in that.

Sidney was just about to read letter number fifteen when he heard the unmistakeable heavy tread on the stairs of Bernie Biddle, who had recently arrived back from burying the Stonehams. It had taken longer than expected because when they tried to place Mrs Stoneham on top, the side of the grave just caved in. They had to wait for the grave diggers to shovel up a new plot into which she went peacefully and alone. Inside Mr Stoneham's coffin his grin was now stretched from ear to ear.

Bernie sat facing Sidney as he waited to regain his breath after his run up the stairs.

''ave a good time last night?'

He spotted the egg-size bruise on the side of Bernie's head. 'Blimey, I hope she didn't do that,' he said, laughing. 'Come on, open up Bernie. Did she show you a good time, or did she whack you for trying to take a liberty, eh?'

'Good time?' said Bernie. 'Good time? Your bloody computer, Mr Bliss, didn't warn me that she was a right nutter.'

'She's a little bit odd, I'll grant you that,' said Sidney. 'But I wouldn't call her a nutter. It's her eyesight, that's all. It's a bit wonky.'

'A bit wonky! Well you'd think she'd be able to see the difference between Mr Stoneham and me.'

'What are you on about, Bernie boy. That bang on your head must have affected your brain.'

'Even I wondered that, Mr Bliss, when I hit it against the coffin. Knocked me out cold, it did. But there was no mistaking what I saw when I came round. It's not every day you see a sight like that. God, it was the most 'orrible thing I'd ever seen.'

''old on, 'old on. Not so quick. You hit your head on a coffin? Where were you? Having a bit of leg over in the Chapel of Rest?'

'No. We were in the back of my hearse. That's where she said she wanted to have it off.'

'*She* suggested it. Blimey, well done mate. Nobody else has even tried to make a move on her. A move away from her, yes. But...'

'She said it was her first date with the agency,' said Bernie.

'Yeah, well she always tells the punter that. It would be a bit off-putting if you knew how many times she has been disappointed. But you obviously switched her on. A great date, mate.'

'But she wanted the date with Mr Stoneham, not me.'

'Do what?'

'That's what I'm telling you. When I came round she was in the coffin rubbing herself all over Mr bloody Stoneham. The embalming wax had hardly even dried on him.'

Sidney felt his mouth opening and shutting like a pensioner's purse. 'Blimey, I had no idea she was like that. Just Charlie Stoneham's luck to get it too late. But at least he was stiff.'

'It's not funny, Mr Bliss. I've never been so shocked or so disappointed in all my life. Thought she really fancied me.'

'I'm sure she did, Bernie. I suppose you got her turned on, then you got yourself knocked out and then she sort of tried to lean over to help you and fell in on top of lucky old Charlie.'

'The Leanover is the only part of that I believe,' said Bernie.

'I must be honest, I didn't know Phoebe was like that,' said Sidney, shaking his head.

'Phoebe who?'

'Scratchitt, of course.'

'Who's she?'

'The girl you went out with last night. Phoebe

63

Scratchitt. Code name Pebble. Dodgy eyes but a warm heart. Likes cats. That Phoebe Scratchitt.'

'Wasn't what she called herself.'

Sidney snapped his fingers. 'Silly me,' he said. 'Phoebe's always changing her name. I think she's Monica Crackitt at the moment.'

Bernie shook his head. 'No, that wasn't her name either.'

Sidney stared into space trying to think of her previous assumed names. 'Mary Muffitt?'

Bernie shook his head.

'Joan Strokeit?'

Bernie shook his head.

'Fiona Feelit?

Bernie shook his head.

'For gawd's sake, Bernie,' Sidney said. 'I haven't got time for a quiz. What was her bloody name last night then?'

'Eileen Overr,' said Bernie.

'Do what?' said Sidney, not believing his ears.

'Eileen Overr. Big knockers, spitting image of the reporter on the *Advertiser* that you're always whistling at.'

Sidney's mouth had now gone from pensioner's purse to opening and shutting like a constipated goldfish.

'But it couldn't have been... it can't have been... I've not let her out of the traps yet.'

'It was,' said Bernie. 'Mrs Bliss got us together last night.'

'Mrs Bliss...?'

A red mist started to come down over his eyes like a

1. Sidney Bliss (Sidney James) has his hands full with Esme Crowfoot (Joan Sims), who was his blind date. *BFI Stills*

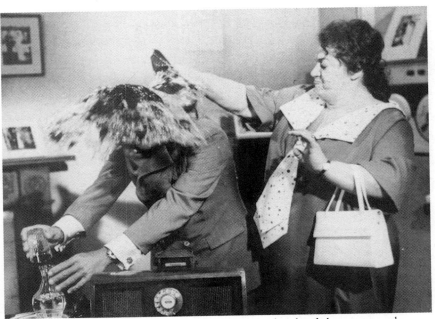

2. Sophie Bliss (Hattie Jacques) cracks open a bottle of champers on the head of her two-timing husband Sidney (Sidney James). *BFI Stills*

3. Bandaged Bertie Muffet (Richard O'Callaghan) loses his head for
Sally Martin (Jacki Piper). *BFI Stills*

4. Terence Philpot (Terry Scott) keeps a date with Jenny Grubb
(Imogen Hassall), who is determined to make him 'altar' his ways. *BFI Stills*

5. Husband-hunting Esme Crowfoot (Joan Sims) is a woman on top with Percival Snooper (Kenneth Williams).

6. All is not bliss in the dating game as Sidney (Sidney James) and Sophie (Hattie Jacques) face the consequences of yet another mismatch.

7. 'There's something come between us,' says Terence Philpot (Terry Scott) as he attempts to carry on with Jenny Grubb (Imogen Hassall). *BFI Stills*

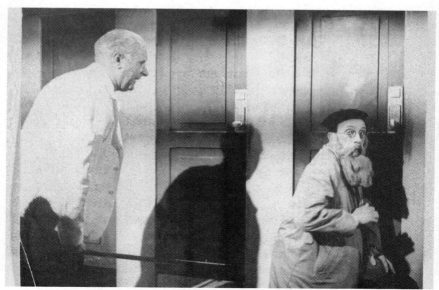

8. Master of disguise James Bedsop (Charles Hawtrey) is caught peeping at an inconvenient place. *BFI Stills*

9. Wrestler 'Gripper' Burke (Bernard Bresslaw) gets to grips with
Percival Snooper (Kenneth Williams), with Miss Dempsey (Patsy Rowlands)
lending a hand.

10. Esme Crowfoot (Joan Sims) is given a lap of honour by 'Gripper' Burke (Bernard Bresslaw).

11. The dating game becomes a dangerous business as Adrian (Julian Holloway) shoots a line with two date mates (Jacki Piper and Lucy Griffiths).

12. Percival Snooper (Kenneth Williams) is shocked to discover that Miss Dempsey (Patsy Rowlands) is the dish

curtain dropping on a bad opening night.

'And you're absolutely and positively sure that she was trying to do the business with Mr Stoneham in the coffin?'

Bernie nodded. 'No doubt about it,' he said. 'She cried like a baby when I pulled her out and put the lid back on.'

Sidney was on his knees under the desk.

'What are you doing there, Mr Bliss?' Bernie asked.

'I'm recovering all the kinky letters,' he said. 'I think I've found them a mate who will prove a great date.'

Sidney worked through until ten putting all the kinky letters, which were the vast majority, in one pile and the straightish ones in another. He may have lost respect for Sheila Blige, but she could still prove a nice big earner for the agency and, hopefully, help him get the bank and the tax men off his back.

When he arrived home two hours later than intended, he found a scribbled note from Sophie:

'Dear Rodney,
    Gone to bed. Your dinner's in the dog. Your blankets are on the sofa. First thing tomorrow I want you to get a refund from the *Advertiser* for the cock-up in the nurse advert.'

'Cock-up?' wondered Sidney aloud. 'What cock-up?'

He rummaged through the newspapers piled on the coffee table and found the previous days *Advertiser* opened at the Lonely Hearts page. Sophie had circled their agency small-ad in red ink. Sidney looked at it once, then twice and a third time before screwing up the paper and throwing it at the dog.

Instead of PALE NURSE SEEKS MAN, it read MALE NURSE SEEKS MAN...

As he lay tossing and turning the night away on the sofa, Sidney suddenly said out loud, 'Who the bleeding hell's Rodney?'

The dog shrugged and sloped out into the kitchen.

5

As SIDNEY had feared, a newspaper reporter imaginative enough and unbalanced enough to climb into a coffin with a corpse knew no restrictions when let loose at the typewriter. The Sheila Blige by-lined front-page splash in the *Advertiser* was a masterpiece of half-truths, innuendo, exaggeration and fabrication.

Sadly, the one who came out of it worst of all was Cedric, the reasonably innocent nightwatchman. Yet from this mess was to grow the greatest money-making idea of Sidney's life.

He read the article sitting alone in his office. Sophie stayed at home writing a chapter for her novel that was entitled 'Murder by Accident'. This followed a row over breakfast in which she had been unjustifiably accused of having an affair with somebody called Rodney.

'You expect me to believe that he's some fictitious character in a book,' said Sidney, 'when I know for a fact that you've been writing notes to him and making him bleedin' porridge. You're always accusing me of trying to get my leg over. Well now I'm the one who's making the accusations, and I won't rest until I've found out who this Rodney geezer is and have given him a punch right on the old bugle.'

He walked out in a huff, leaving Sophie day-dreaming up ways that a husband could be killed by what would look like accidental death. Her two favourites so far were electrocution while in the bath and falling off the roof while fixing the television aerial. 'Now how,' she typed, 'can I convince ~~Sidney~~ Rodney that he should go up on to the roof?'

What she could have done with is Sheila Blige's vivid imagination (which would one day win for her the Investigative Reporter of the Year award during a long and distasteful career in Fleet Street). Her story was headlined:

DATE MATES IN CEMETERY ORGY

And there was a sub-head that read:

GATEKEEPER ON THE TAKE

AS HE MASTERMINDS LUST

AMONG THE GRAVESTONES

The article was accompanied by photographs of Sheila and Bernie, both with their faces masked out, appearing to be tumbling around in the back of the hearse. Sidney was relieved to find that she at least kept her word about not using real names. Bernie was called Bill Burns, and Sidney appeared very well disguised as Sidney Blissett, and described as 'the greedy, grasping proprietor of a dating agency that preys on the loneliness and vulnerability of innocent people in search of love and companionship.'

There was a snatched picture of poor old Cedric 'stuffing' the pound note handed over by Ralph into his pocket, and a caption that read: 'Cemetery gatekeeper Cedric Dedham collects his wages of sin as he prepares to throw the graveyard open to more sex-crazed ghouls.' A self-taken photograph showed Ralph holding aloft his false left arm, with a caption that read: 'When

68

he was confronted, the gatekeeper tried to tear our photographer limb from limb."

Sidney was slumped in despair at his desk after reading the article. In more than twenty years ducking and diving for a living he had never felt so low, well certainly not since his time-share caravan-holidays idea had sunk when he had over-booked to five families at once. They had all insisted on getting into the one caravan he owned in Margate, and it had collapsed under their weight. It cost him five thousand pounds in compensation, and the caravan had become compressed scrap metal. He had a pair of earrings made from the remains which he had given to Sophie in the days when she was the light of his life.

Now here he was with his dating business facing bankruptcy because of all the free love being given away, and his marriage being forced on to the rocks by a geezer called Rodney. He silently cursed the day he had thought of the dating agency scam. 'I wish I could undate it,' he said aloud to himself as he sat in a sea of despondency.

'Yes, undate it,' he repeated for no real reason. Then he said it again, 'Undate it.' He stood up and started to walk round the office trying to keep up with a suddenly racing brain. 'Undate it,' he said, once more with feeling.

'That's it,' he thought, laughing almost crazily to himself, 'I'll start an *undating* agency.'

'For those of you who worry about such things, it should be pointed out that Cedric kept his job at the Council-run graveyard. He knew too much about the Mayor's secret late-night trysts at the cemetery.

Sidney took the telephone off the hook, locked the door and spent the rest of the day putting flesh on what had been a skeletal idea. 'How many husbands,' he thought, 'are locked in loveless marriages? They watch all the single fellers having the time of their lives in this new age of sexual revolution, and what do they get? "Leave me alone, I've got a headache." What they are crying out for is advice on how to escape from the prison into which they have been led by the nose, or, more appropriately, by their private parts. People only got married in our day to get their things together. Now they're being allowed to do it with no strings, or knicker elastic, attached.'

What was needed, he decided, was an 'undating' agency that would give advice on how to get a divorce and how to *untie* the knot. It would operate in reverse to a dating agency, with a prime objective of breaking couples apart rather than bringing them together.

Sidney realised that he could not operate alone. He needed two partners. The first would have to be somebody with experience of being a marriage guidance counsellor, who would be able to reverse all his advice so that he could counsel on divorce rather than marriage. The second would have to be a private detective who could surreptitiously collect any necessary evidence that would speed up divorce proceedings so that their clients could get into the free love swim as quickly as possible.

Doodling with a pencil, Sidney jotted down possible names for the agency, crossing the first nine out and then settling for the tenth:

70

~~THE-BREAKING-UP-IS-EASY-TO-DO-UNDATING-AGENCY~~
~~THE-BROKEN-HEARTS-UNDATING-AGENCY~~
~~THE-NOOKIE-NOOKIE-NOO-UNDATING-AGENCY~~
~~THE-ESCAPE-FROM-HELL-UNDATING-AGENCY~~
~~THE-THIS-WAY-OUT-UNDATING-AGENCY~~
~~THE-FREEDOM-RESTORED-UNDATING-AGENCY~~
~~THE-DIVORCE-MADE-EASY-UNDATING-AGENCY~~
~~THE-KISS-AND-BREAK-UP-UNDATING-AGENCY~~
~~THE-MAKE-WAR-NOT-LOVE-UNDATING-AGENCY~~
THE UNDATING AGENCY

'That's the one,' said Sidney, underlining The Undating Agency. 'Straight, simple and conveys what the agency will be all about.'

He picked up the telephone and made three calls. The first was to Sophie to tell her that he would not be home for a few days. 'I want to have a complete re-think about our lives together,' he said. 'I'm going to shack up in the office. The couch there is more comfortable than the one at home.'

'Suits me fine,' she said, slamming down the telephone and returning in a flood of tears to her typewriter and the sentence, 'She balanced the radio, which was broadcasting *Sports Report*, on the side of the bath and shouted to ~~Rodney~~ Sidney that she had run the water for him.'

The second call was to Percival Snooper, who ran the marriage counsel advice bureau two doors away over the fish and chip shop.

'Percival, Sidney Bliss,' he said.

71

'Oooh, the man who ruined my life,' said Snooper in his peculiar nasal whine.

'You still haven't forgiven me for getting you married, 'ave you?' said Sidney.

'And why should I?' he whined. 'I was as happy as a canine with two tails when I was single. Now I feel as miserable as a castrated cat. All because of being stupid enough to join your silly dating agency.'

'That's what I'm calling you about.'

'I paid your bills in full, inexplicably exorbitant though they were.'

'No, it's not money I'm after. It's you I want.'

'Don't tell me you're coming out of the closet, Sidney Bliss? That would be bliss for some, I'm sure. Nothing surprises me nowadays. I was only saying to my friend Sandy the other day, "Sandy," I said, "I don't know what the world is coming to, I really don't. I had a couple came in to see me this week, with the wife complaining because he did it to her against the freezer. I said that I could not see what the problem was, and she said that because of it they had been banned from the supermarket." I really don't know what the world is coming to, I really don't.'

'Yes, quite, Percival,' said Sidney. 'The reason I'm calling is to ask whether you would be interested in joining me in a new and exciting business venture. It would mean you having to give up the marriage guidance business.'

'Give it up? That's a symphony to my ears. You don't know what I go through here day after day after day, week after week after week listening to moans, groans

72

and nit-picking, fault-finding grouses from couples who simply need their heads knocking together.'

'I won't tell you what my plan is over the blower,' Sidney said, 'You never know who's listening in. But just rest assured I can show you a way out of your rut.'

'Rut?' scoffed Percival. 'I'm not in a rut. I'm stuck up to my Adam's apple in a great big suffocating crevice.'

'Right,' said Sidney, 'let's talk in the 3Ps at seven o'clock.'

'Oooh, I'll have to telephone home to get permission. Her Ladyship wanted me home early tonight to cut her toenails. I'll just tell her that I am having to work late at the office trying to repair a broken marriage. I just wish somebody could show me how to break my one up.'

'Don't worry,' said Sidney, ''elp is at 'and.'

He then prepared to call the James Bedsop Private Detective Agency that was above the jewellers' opposite, now minus the Stonehams. This was a one-man sleuthing business that concentrated on debt collecting, lost moggy tracing and the occasional tailing of straying husbands or their spouses. Sophie often hired him to keep track of Sidney's movements, but he was so incompetent that Sidney became sorry for him and used to give him a lift wherever he went. Bedsop would tuck himself uncomfortably low down behind the driver's seat just so that he could at least tell his client that he had managed to stay out of sight. In return, he would split Sophie's fee with Sidney.

Even giving the always rain-coated, bespectacled Bedsop a lift did not necessarily work for the defective detective. There was one occasion when he had climbed into the back of the wrong car and had been driven to Newcastle before he realised, and then there was the time when he forgot where Sidney had parked. He spent an afternoon walking around a multi-storey car park looking for the unmistakable red Jaguar XK120, and it was several hours before he remembered that on this particular day they had travelled by bus.

His absolute classic, the talk and the laugh of the Pleasant Pheasant Plucker for months, had been when he was hired by the landlord, George Drinkwater, to follow his wife whom he suspected of getting up to some hanky panky. Bedsop got his brief just slightly muddled, and spent a month following *Mr* Drinkwater. He then gave a full report to *Mrs* Drinkwater, who was provided with enough evidence to take her husband for nearly every penny that he had. But he was the only private detective that Sidney knew, and so he made the call.

'Bedsop, James Bedsop. Private dick,' came the answering voice in Sidney's ear. He appeared to have picked up a cross between a Sean Connery and a Humphrey Bogart accent since Sidney had last spoken to him.

'James. Sidney Bliss.'

'This is not James Sidney Bliss. This is Bedsop. James Bedsop. Private dick.'

'No, James. Listen. I am Sidney Bliss. Remember, you used to take lifts in the back of my Jag.'

'I plead the Fifth on the grounds that anything I say may incriminate me.'

74

Sidney looked to the ceiling in exasperation. 'Now listen, James, I need to talk to you.'

'Is it a case?'

'Could be a lot of cases.'

'Have you tried the London Transport lost property office? They have many cases, umbrellas and coats handed in. If you find it there, that will be a fee of ten shillings for my detection work.'

'I haven't lost a case,' said Sidney.

'What have you lost then?'

'Nothing,' said Sidney, wanting to add 'but you've lost your marbles.'

'So why are you wasting my time?'

'I have a business proposition to put to you.'

'What sort of business?'

'Private detective work.'

'Well you've come to the right man. This is Bedsop. James Bedsop. Private dick.'

'Right, let's start again.'

'Start what again?'

'Giving you my reason for calling.'

'When did you call? Did you leave a message?'

'I'm calling now, for gawd's sake.'

'I know you are. But what about the last call?'

'I've not made any previous calls.'

'Then how did I know where your car was for the lifts?'

'At last, James, you remember me. Sidney Bliss.'

'Of course I remember you. Red Jaguar XK120, twin cam six-cylinder three point four litre engine. Not a lot of room behind the driver's seat.'

'That's the one. I want you to help me with a business venture.'

'Well you know the way I work,' Bedsop said, dropping into his Humphrey Bogart/Sam Spade speak. 'Time's money. I charge by the hour. A dollar an hour, and all the black coffee I can drink. I don't come cheap, but I'm good at what I do. I'll shake down blackmailers, slap a few hoodlums around and snoop into places where the cops won't risk getting their nostrils dirty. Am I hired?'

'Let's discuss it tonight in the Pleasant Pheasant Plucker at seven,' said Sidney.

'Out of bounds,' said Bedsop. 'A client there has some unfinished business with me.'

Sidney laughed. 'You're not banned any more,' he said. 'George Drinkwater now thinks it was the best day's work of his life when he got rid of his missus. And he's got you to thank for it.'

'I just do what I have to do,' said Bedsop. 'I'll be there at seven. Alone, because that's the way I like it.'

As Sidney replaced the receiver he seriously wondered whether James Bedsop had not investigated a crime too many.

Sidney had just one thing to do before going to the Pleasant Pheasant Plucker. He slipped quietly into the car park at the back of the office which he shared with Bodie and Co and the *Advertiser* staff. Hidden beneath his jacket he had a length of wire cable.

After making sure there were no prying eyes, he ducked down beside the Rover parked in the editor's space and tied one end of the cable to the front bumper. He then tied the opposite end to the back wheel of an MV Augusta 350cc motorbike that was parked two bays away.

He would save his revenge on Sheila Blige for another time, another place. Cuban-heeled Ralph would do for now. He would have liked to have torn him limb from limb. On behalf of Cedric.

Sidney returned to his office and watched from the back window. He wondered which of them would be leaving first, Ralph or the editor.

He felt as if the tide of luck was beginning to turn in his favour when he saw them walk into the car park together.

Ralph, gravel rash prominent on his face, kick started his motorbike while the editor was still settling himself into the driver's seat in his Rover. As the photographer revved up for his usual roaring start, the motorbike reared, and Ralph was thrown to the ground. Even more satisfying for the watching Sidney was a loud metal-cracking sound as the bumper was dragged off the front of the editor's Rover.

Ralph's face was a picture.

6

THE SALOON BAR of the Pleasant Pheasant Plucker was virtually deserted when Sidney arrived at ten to seven. He handed his keys to landlord George Drinkwater, who was trapped in a corner by the amateur soothsayer Ivor Bodie, who was in full flow on the subject of healthy eating.

'Mark my words,' he was saying in time to his clicking and clacking teeth, 'there will come a day very soon when the government will 'ave to hadmit that we should not be eating meat of any description. Take it from me, it's what drives people mad. Our secret service agents poisoned Hitler, y'know. They slipped a plate of British roast beef into the kitchen in his bunker. He scoffed the lot and went so mad that he ordered the invasion of Russia. The German women on his staff also hate some, and they started acting so strangely that Hitler's personal physician was called in and he diagnosed that they were suffering from Mad Fraus Disease.'

There was not even a pause for breath as he continued talking in a monotone voice that could have been the prototype for the speaking clock. 'Here's another fascinating fact for you to digest,' he said, 'Nearly hevery person that I've buried over the past forty odd years has been a meat eater. Now surely that proves something...'

Sidney escaped to the far side of the bar where Nancy

served him with a pint of bitter, and gave him 7p change from the 25p that he put on the counter. 'I don't know,' he said, shaking his head. 'I remember when you could have a pint and a packet of fags and still have change from two bob.'

Nancy leant over the bar and beckoned Sidney to come closer. This he did reluctantly because she had been known to suck men in and blow them out in bubbles from that range. 'Did you get my application for the chap you advertised?' she asked in a loud whisper. 'You know, in the *Advertiser*.'

'What, the male nurse?'

'No, silly. He was advertising for men. No I mean the one who wanted a nice buxom barmaid.'

She thrust herself across the bar with such vigour that Sidney was in danger of having his eyes knocked out. 'They don't come much more buxom than me,' she added, quite unnecessarily. 'An old boyfriend once told me that Alf Ramsey would have selected me for England if he had been picking a Big Knockers eleven. So come on, Sidney, who's the lucky bloke in the newspaper advertisement whose going to get his hands on my two treasures?'

'I don't think you will be so keen, Nancy, when I tell you the name of the client.'

'I'm virtually impossible to disappoint where men are concerned,' she said.

'It's Bernie Biddle,' Sidney said.

'Oh, I *am* disappointed,' Nancy said, pulling a face. 'Blimey, I wouldn't want him baked, boiled, roasted or poached. He spends half his time rubbing embalming fluid on dead bodies. I like my men to give me a nice slow massage with lots of oil and talcum powder, but having his hands on me would just give me the creeps. I mean, you'd be wondering where his hands had been before, wouldn't you?' She gave a cackling laugh. 'Mind you, some men I've been with have been just like corpses, only not so stiff if you follow me. I can imagine Bernie being like that. He's always with a corpse when he's on the job.'

The mention of Bernie prompted Sidney to interrupt Ivor Bodie's dissertation on the likelihood of Martians landing on Earth within the next decade. 'Seen the *Advertiser* today, Mr Bodie?' he asked.

'Seen it, read it, dissected it,' Bodie replied. 'There's an undertaker's assistant somewhere bringing shame to our profession, and I have to say, with no disrespect to you, Mr Blissett...'

'Bliss,' corrected Sidney. 'Mr Bliss.'

But the correction went unacknowledged as Bodie, a conversation road hog, motored on without any attempt to give way.

'...that the dating agency business didn't come out of it too well, either. I went to see Cedric straight away after reading the article, and he said it was so dark he couldn't be sure who it was. Somebody had the temerity to say that the bloke in the picture with a mask on looked like my Bernie Biddle. I told them not to be daft because I know for a fact that Bernie was out on the road at the time taking Mr Stoneham for a nice peaceful drive. He needed some space away from Mrs Stoneham. There were bad vibrations passing between the two of

80

them. When you've been in the business as long as I have you feel that sort of thing. I thought it best to give them a break from each other.'

He adjusted his top plate, which had been in danger of dropping into his whisky glass. 'I hope you wouldn't tolerate any of those weirdo clients on your books, Mr Blisset,' he said. 'It's all a sign of the falling standards in hour society. You mark my words, it won't be long before we have pictures on the front pages of hour national newspapers, not local rags like the *Advertiser*, showing hour royalty 'aving their toes sucked and cabinet ministers getting hinvolved in similar unhealthy practices. The place is going to the dogs, take it from me...'

Sidney switched off from him, and the seemingly remote-controlled Bodie continued to talk away to himself. The landlord had long since left him to serve in the other bar. He was so engrossed in what he was saying to himself that he did not notice his assistant Bernie Biddle sneaking in for a swift half before returning to his embalming duties.

'You were lucky,' said Sidney, passing him his drink. 'Cedric didn't recognise you.'

'Lucky my foot,' said Bernie. 'It cost me a tenner to buy his silence. Now I want my deposit refunded, Mr Bliss. That's hard-earned money that is, and I've not had so much as a grope.'

'Don't despair, Bernie,' he said. 'I'm going to let you have, free and gratis, a date mate who will be absolutely perfect for you. Her name is Phoebe Scratchitt, and she's right up your street.'

'You mean she lives in the same street as what I do?' said Bernie.

'No, that's just a figure of speech,' said Sidney. 'What I mean is that she will really suit you.'

'You mentioned her the last time we talked, and said she was always changing her name.'

'Oh, no,' lied Sidney. 'Not that Phoebe. This is another client. She won't want to go to the cemetery with you. She's full of life this one.'

'I had a tumble against a tombstone once,' said Nancy. 'I was married at the time, and when I got home my old man was in bed. I was undressing when he said, "Where have you been?" I said, "Out for a drink with the girls." As I was walking away from him towards the bathroom looking my best in the altogether, he said, "How come after all this time I've been married to you I never knew about that tattoo on your bum?" I said, "What are you on about," and he said, "Well, according to your bum you died in 1876".'

'I don't get it,' said Bernie.

'It was the imprint from the gravestone,' explained Nancy. 'Wouldn't mind another graveyard grind.'

'I don't think Cedric would let us in,' said Bernie.

'Uh, it was just a figure of speech,' she said quickly, and went and stood listening to Bodie rather than risk being chatted up by a zombie.

'...and mark my words, the day will come sooner than you think when the Berlin Wall will come down and Communism in Europe will be as dead as the Dodo,' he was saying. 'And potatoes won't come by the pound but they will be kilos.'

'Coo,' said Nancy, 'won't it be odd asking for three pounds of kilos.'

Sidney was relieved to see Percival Snooper come into the bar as Bernie went out after sinking his half pint. 'What will you have, Percival, my old china?' he said, greeting him with a warm handshake. It was like shaking hands with a piece of wet fish.

'Just a glass of water, please,' Snooper said. 'Can't let her Ladyship smell alcohol on my breath. She would have a fit.'

'Hello, Mr Snooper,' said Nancy, flashing him a bright smile and a panoramic view of her greatest assets. 'Haven't seen you in months. Been away?'

'Yes, you could say that,' said Snooper. 'I've been in a sort of open prison.'

'Oh dear,' said Nancy. 'What did you do wrong?'

'I did the most serious thing I could have done. I got married.'

Sidney led him to a table in the far corner of the bar. 'We'll be joined by the redoubtable James Bedsop soon,' he said.

'Not the private detective?'

'The same one.'

'Are you trusting him to find this place on his own?' said Snooper, tossing his Macintosh on to the coat stand alongside the table. 'He does some occasional work for the marriage guidance bureau. Last time we used him all he had to do was simply hand a legal writ to somebody who had walked out on his wife. He handed his umbrella to the husband, and went home with the writ.'

'He'll be all right for the sort of work needed in the new business venture I want to discuss with you,' said Sidney. 'He claims to have become much better at following people and says he has now become a master of disguise. Anyway, forget him. Let me tell you why I asked you to meet me.'

'I'm all ears. What's the great plan?'

'An undating agency,' said Sidney.

Snooper looked at him blankly. 'I beg your pardon?'

'An undating agency, where couples go to untie the knot.'

'Stop mucking about,' said Snooper, a slow grin spreading across his face to signal that he knew when he was having his leg pulled. 'Come on, you're having me on. What do you *really* want to talk about?'

'That's it,' said Sidney. 'An undating agency. I promise you it's a winner of an idea.'

He spent the next thirty minutes going all the way through the plan with Snooper, whose early scepticism turned first to incredulity and then to crackling enthusiasm.

'This is the most brilliant idea since the wheel,' he said. 'There's hardly a married man that I know who does not want to escape. They want to drop out not only from marriage but also from all the miseries that go with it, like mortgages, menstruation and mother-in-laws.'

'That will make a great slogan,' said Sidney, moving a hand through the air as he read an imaginary billboard: PUT THE MISERY OF MORTGAGES, MENSTRUATION AND MOTHER-IN-LAWS BEHIND YOU. JOIN THE UNDATING AGENCY.

84

'When can we start?' said Snooper, so excited that he decided to celebrate with a whisky. ('Just a small one.')

'I think we should start as soon as possible,' Sidney said. 'I'll put an advertisement in the *Advertiser* tomorrow, and we will be able to judge by the response if there is a market for an undating agency.'

'A market?' said Snooper. 'There's not just a market. There's a whole army of men out there wanting to be free and back to their single days when they could do as they please, go where they please and please who they please. All you have to do is look around this bar for the potential customers, and then multiply it by every pub in the land.'

The bar had become crowded since they had sat down to start talking. Sidney could tell at a glance the men who were desperate to break away from their old mundane existence and tired, boring image. It was written all over them in the way they had started dressing, husbands of thirty plus years of age and trying too hard to look like the youngsters they were constantly deriding.

Standing at the bar Sidney could count half a dozen likely clients, all of them with ridiculously flared trousers, multi-patterned shirts with matching kipper ties, thick leather belts straining round spreading stomachs and what was left of their hair bubble permed and reaching down to their shoulders. He himself had always fought against this trend towards the well-groomed hippy look. It was not out of place on the icons of the age like Georgie Best, Charlie George and Kevin Keegan or the so-called singers who wiggled their bottoms and hit bum notes on *Top of the Pops* every week. But on these men galloping towards middle-age it looked ridiculous, and delivered a screamed-out message that they wanted to break away from the chains of convention in general and the restraints of marriage in particular.

'You're right, Percival,' said Sidney. 'The pubs and clubs of Great Britain are heaving with men who want to become undated. You can also spot them on any dance floor, men looking complete prats twisting and shouting without a partner near them when all they've previously ever done is the hokey cokey.'

'Have you noticed that we keep talking about husbands but never wives,' said Snooper. 'There's an extremely big trade to be had with them as well, I can tell you. You should hear some of the things they say when they come to me for counselling. Oooh, you wouldn't believe it. Just last week I had a wife try to have her way with me in my office. I had to hide under the desk to escape her advances. I tried to put her off by biting her ankles, but all that did was turn her on even more.'

He paused for a quick tilt at his whisky glass. 'In the end I had to climb out of the window to escape her clutches,' he continued. 'She was like a mad woman consumed with desire for my body. All because she's not getting nookie at home. She is totally representative of the thousands of wives who want to break away from the drudgery of married life. They want their freedom just as much as we do, but they're all scared to make the break. They're clinging on to the life raft called marriage as if it's the be-all-and-end-all. What rubbish. Marriage is the most evil human rights invasion ever perpetrated by the establishment to keep free-thinking individuals under the thumb and to stop them thinking independently.'

'It's true what you say about the wives,' said Sidney, trying to get his head round the fact that the man he was talking to was a marriage guidance counsellor by profession. 'But I think we should concentrate on the unhappy 'usbands first. We'll try to get round to the wives later. Let's be honest, that's a world no man can hope to fathom. As long as I've got a hole where the sun never shines, I will never understand the way that my wife's mind works. She is on another planet. D'you know something, she's having a fling at the moment with a geezer called Rodney, and is trying to convince me that it's all in her mind rather than in mine. It's driving me out of my mind, I can tell you. It has reached the stage where I am thinking of taking a leaf out of her book, and putting a private detective on her trail.'

This thought reminded Sidney that James Bedsop was supposed to have joined them, and just as he was wondering where Bedsop had got to, the coat stand started to move towards them. A raincoated, bespectacled figure emerged from beneath the mountain of coats.

'Hi, you guys,' he said in a pseudo-American accent. 'I'm Bedsop. James Bedsop. Private dick.'

Snooper was so shocked by Bedsop's dramatic appearance that he ordered another whisky. 'Make it a large one,' he said.

'Frightened the life out of us,' said Sidney. ''ow long you been hiding there?'

'Since ten minutes before you came in.'

'So you've heard all about the plan?'

'What plan's that?'

'The one I've just outlined to Percival.'

'Oh, goodness no. I couldn't hear a flipping thing through all those coats and things. Had a sleeve stuffed in my ears most of the time.'

'So what was the point of staying hidden for so long?' Sidney asked.

'I fell asleep,' said Bedsop. 'I've been burning the midnight oil on a highly confidential case.'

He peered around looking for anybody eavesdropping. 'Did you know,' he confided, 'that the Mayor of our great borough is having a secret liason with Marjorie Marshmallow.'

'What, the hairdresser in the high street, peroxide-blonde with a big mole on her face?' said Sidney.

'That's the one. The Mayoress is paying me two pounds an hour to keep tabs on him, but of course I am not at liberty to discuss the case. I would never dream of breaking my client's confidentiality.'

Nancy was standing by the table, having brought over three drinks. 'These are with the compliments of the landlord, Mr Drinkwater,' she said. 'And he says to thank Mr Bedsop for his freedom, and he wishes him luck with the Mayor's case.'

She put the drinks on the table. 'Incidentally,' she added, looking at Bedsop, 'Margie gave the Mayor the elbow weeks ago. He's now having it off with Mrs

Tway, the almoner at the hospital.'

'Ah,' said Bedsop, scribbling a pencilled note on a beer mat, 'that explains why he's not made an appearance at the hairdressers. I've been hiding in the salon every night this week disguised as an overhead hair dryer.'

Sidney spent the next hour explaining the undating agency plan to Bedsop, who had the disconcerting habit of switching chairs every five minutes because he said he did not want to give anybody the chance 'to get a bead' on him.

He dropped into Bogart speak to sum up his feelings about the idea, and his part in it as the chief investigator on behalf of clients. 'Of all the joints in all the towns, I had to walk into this one,' he said. 'I'm sure glad I did because this idea is gonna knock 'em stiff.'

He raised his glass. 'Here's looking at you, kids.'

His two new partners responded by draining their glasses. Snooper, who had stopped drinking the day he got married, then fell off his chair dead drunk.

Sidney passed the Pleasant Pheasant Plucker car keys test, and ran Snooper home in his Jaguar. He then discovered just why Snooper was so keen to tunnel his way out of his marriage.

Mrs Snooper, in dressing-gown, slippers and curlers, was waiting at the door when Sidney helped Percival up the garden drive of their semi-detached house. She quickly gauged her husband's condition and, grim-faced like a prison warden on death row, she indicated for Sidney to take him down the side of the house towards a garden shed.

89

Moving quickly behind them, Mrs Snooper collected the garden hosepipe and turned on the tap before Sidney realised what she was planning. They were just short of the garden shed when the stream of water hit them. Both Percival and Sidney were soaked through to the skin before Mrs Snooper threw the hosepipe at them and then stormed into the house, bolting the door behind her.

Sidney helped Percival find some sacking to lay on, and then drove himself back to his office for a night on the couch and to consider his plans for launching the undating agency that would most likely have Percival Snooper as its first client.

Inside the almoner's office at the local hospital, a filing cabinet coughed. James Bedsop, private dick, was on the case.

7

> ATTENTION ALL FED-UP HUSBANDS
>
> DO YOU WANT HELP GETTING OUT OF THE TANGLED
> WEB YOU WEAVED WHEN YOU MADE THE FATAL
> MISTAKE OF GETTING MARRIED? WE CAN SHOW YOU
> THE WAY TO FREEDOM AND PUT YOU ON THE ROAD
> BACK TO A SINGLE LIFE AND THE HAPPINESS
> YOU ONCE KNEW. WRITE NOW FOR FULL DETAILS
> SENT IN STRICTEST CONFIDENCE TO...
> THE UNDATING AGENCY BOX 6969

SIDNEY SENSED that he had tapped an oil well when two compositors, the advertising sales supervisor and a typesetter on the *Advertiser* hand-delivered letters before the newspaper had even hit the streets. He himself had selected the 6969 box office number because he thought that, figuratively speaking, it gave the advertisement that little bit of extra spice. He knew that he could be on to something when the married woman on the order counter refused to take the copy and insisted that her male supervisor deal with it. But it was not until the next morning's first post that he wondered just how big a gusher he had struck.

Following a restless night on the back office couch, he had just fallen off into a deep sleep when he was awakened by a knocking that was so loud, it felt as if it was in his head. It slowly dawned on him through the cobwebs of sleep smothering his brain that it was the front door that was being banged, and he stumbled into the front office and opened the window. When he looked down he saw Ivor Bodie, all dressed in his refinery ready to see a client off, crashing at the door with the silver top end of his funeral walking stick. He was knee-deep in sacks of mail.

'Get down 'ere and clear this lot out of the way immediately,' Bodie roared in a voice fit to wake the dead. 'I've got to get Mr Fotheringale to his funeral.'

'I'll be right down,' shouted Sidney, waking up to the fact that he had actually stumbled on to an idea that seemed to have worked in a spectacular fashion that was beyond his wildest dreams. Goodbye bankruptcy and two fingers to the tax man. He had gone down two flights of stairs before he realised that he was still in his vest and underpants, and quickly ran back up and threw on his clothes.

'What is all this?' demanded Bodie, waving his stick at the sacks of mail like a demented Toscanini as Sidney emerged on the pavement blinking in the morning sunlight. 'You've not gone into that porn lark, 'ave you? I won't stand for that. This is a funeral parlour not a Soho clip joint. That sort of thing would give my clients the shock of their lives.'

Sidney was pushing the sacks to one side of the doorway. 'It's got nothing to do with porn or sleaze,' he said. 'I'm just going to start helping husbands break out of the prison of marriage.'

Bodie's jaw dropped, and his face became longer than Nijinsky's (the 1970 Derby winner, not the ballet dancer). 'It's a bit bloody late to tell me that now,' he moaned. 'Thirty-nine ruddy years I've done, and not a day off for good behaviour. That's a longer sentence than even the Great Train Robbers got.'

'It's never too late to make the break, Mr Bodie,' said Sidney with the enthusiasm of a spreader of the gospel. 'That will be one of our main selling points. No matter how long you've been a prisoner, you can still break free from the shackles.'

'What a load of bollocks,' said Mr Bodie, and stomped off to prepare Mr Fotheringale for his final journey. Sidney had never heard him swear before and felt himself gaping. This time it was *his* teeth that were in danger of falling out.

It took him an hour to get the six sacks of mail up the stairs to his office, mainly due to a thirty minute hold-up when he and the fourth sack got stuck solid in the doorway with Bernie, who was backing out with the departing Mr Fotheringale laid out in his coffin. He heard Mr Bodie swear for a second time when it was decided that the only way to make room for them both was to remove the front door frame.

'We'll need a chippie,' said Bodie.

'He don't open until eleven o'clock,' said Bernie. 'And he don't start frying until twelve.'

'I mean a carpenter, you idiot,' said Bodie, his teeth performing a war dance. He sent an assistant off to find one, and meantime decided to see what he could do himself with a crowbar from his workshop.

'Don't forget my date with Phoebe Scratchitt,' Bernie said, while Bodie worked around them preparing to free them to go their separate ways.

'Call in to see me after you've laid Mr Fotheringale

to rest,' said Sidney, 'and I'll make the dream date contact for you.'

Nobody was quite sure how it happened, but Bodie – balancing precariously on a step-ladder – should have been getting the end of the crowbar inside the wooden frame around the door. Instead – possibly by force of habit – he somehow managed to get it hooked under the lid of the coffin, and as he prised with a sudden downward thrust of his right arm the lid lifted and slid to the left. The pressure of the crowbar on the front of the coffin tipped it forward and an unseeing, unfeeling, undignified Mr Fotheringale suddenly sat up, banging his head on the top of the door frame.

'That must have given him the fright of his life,' said Sidney, seeing the funny side, despite the burden of the mailbag across his shoulders. 'I bet he'll have a headache in the morning.'

A fuming Bodie was not amused. He levered his client back into his wooden overcoat with a combination of the crowbar and his walking stick, and then barked: 'Come on, otherwise Mr Fotheringale will be late for his own funeral.'

Once back in his office, Sidney suffered one of the biggest disappointments of his life. Each bag that he had manhandled upstairs was stuffed with more letters addressed to the non-existent male nurse. He was just about to call Percival Snooper and tell him the idea was a flop when the second post arrived. This time there were ten sacks, each containing seven hundred and fifty letters, and all seven thousand seven hundred and fifty of them were from fed-up husbands.

Even Mr Fotheringale, belatedly on his way to the cemetery, would have heard Sidney's cry of 'Eureka!'

Snooper was nursing a black eye when he arrived at Sidney's office in response to an excited call within two minutes of the second post being vetted. 'How did you get that?' asked Sidney. 'You didn't have a mark on you when I left you last night.'

'It was her Ladyship, wasn't it,' Snooper explained, catching his breath after the four-flight climb. It would doubtless have killed him if he had had to help bring up the mail bags, particularly the fourth sack that inexplicably caused the traffic jam.

'She gave you that?' said Sidney. 'Blimey, my Rhinobottomed missus wouldn't dare lay a finger on me.'

'Oh, she didn't do anything as crude as strike me with her fists,' said Snooper. 'All I did was ask for a hard-boiled egg for breakfast and she threw it across the kitchen at me. Hit me right in the eye.'

'Blimey,' said Sidney, chuckling. 'Bet you were shell shocked.'

'It's no laughing matter. That for me was the final straw. I have decided that I, Percival Clapham Junction Snooper, will be the first client of The Undating Agency.'

'Clapham Junction?' said Sidney.

'It was where I was conceived, apparently,' said Snooper. 'The family story is that my father was railroaded into marriage. He would have jumped at the chance of using our agency.'

'Right,' said Sidney in a businesslike manner, 'we

must now decide how we're going to cash in on this little lot.' He nodded towards the piles of letters. Many of them, Sidney had noticed, were from the same writers of the letters to the male nurse.

'What fees should we charge for our services?' asked Snooper.

'I think a ten pound enrolment fee, and then a further payment of fifteen pounds once their divorce has become absolute,' said Sidney.

'What will they get for their ten pounds?'

'We will send them the Undating Agency Ten Commandments, and a list of our expert extra services all of which will be on offer at just five pounds a time.'

'Ten Commandments?' said Snooper. 'What are they?'

Sidney fished several sheets of paper out of his drawer on which he had scribbled notes during his long, restless night. 'This is what I suggest we have typed out and then photocopied,' he said, handing the following list to Snooper:

THE UNDATING AGENCY TEN COMMANDMENTS

1. THOU SHALT PLEDGE TO MAKE THE BREAK FROM YOUR WIFE WITHIN ONE YEAR OF ENROLLING AS A MEMBER.
2. THOU SHALT LOVE THY NEIGHBOUR OR ANYBODY ELSE'S NEIGHBOUR IF YOU FEEL LIKE IT.
3. THOU SHALT RESOLUTELY REFUSE TO DO ANY MORE ODD JOBS OR DECORATING AROUND THE HOUSE.
4. THOU SHALT INSIST ON NIGHTS OUT WITH THE BOYS (OR GIRLS) WHENEVER YOU FANCY IT.

5. THOU SHALT BAR ENTRY TO YOUR HOME OF THE MOTHER-IN-LAW, UNLESS SHE AGREES TO SIGN A DECLARATION OF TOTAL SILENCE.

6. THOU SHALT TAKE HOLIDAYS SEPARATE FROM YOUR WIFE AND BEHAVE JUST LIKE A SINGLE MAN AS PRACTICE FOR YOUR FUTURE FREEDOM.

7. THOU SHALT CUT YOUR WIFE'S CLOTHES ALLOWANCE TO A BARE MINIMUM AND DIP INTO YOUR POCKET ONLY TO IMPROVE YOUR OWN WARDROBE.

8. THOU SHALT NEVER EVER GO SHOPPING WITH YOUR WIFE, UNLESS IT'S TO KEEP A BRAKE ON HER SPENDING.

9. THOU SHALT DEMAND THAT YOUR WIFE OBEYS YOU AT ALL TIMES AND ALWAYS PUTS YOUR NEEDS FIRST UNTIL THE SEPARATION AND/OR DIVORCE.

10. THOU SHALT TAKE FULL ADVANTAGE OF THE AGENCY'S EXTRA SERVICES TO SPEED THE MOMENT OF FREEDOM.

Snooper finished reading them, and puffed out his cheeks. 'Phew,' he said, 'they will take some keeping. Take the fifth commandment, for instance. My mother-in-law would eat me alive if I tried to bar her from our home, particularly as she paid the deposit so that we could get a manageable mortgage. And as for getting her to sign a declaration of silence, that will be like trying to switch off Niagara Falls.'

'I'm not saying that agency members should stick to all ten commandments,' said Sidney. 'After all, how many of us follow all of the proper Commandments. I've tried loving my neighbour, but she keeps blanking me every time I make a pass.'

'What about these extra services?' asked Snooper.

'Just exactly what will they be?'

'Well, personal advice from you for a start,' Sidney explained. 'You can tell them how to get under the wife's skin with annoying habits and how to give grounds for divorce by getting involved in some hanky panky. They must be taught that a bit on the side is a must rather than just a luxury.'

'You mean you want me to tell them the exact opposite of what I do as a marriage guidance counsellor?' asked Snooper.

'You've got it in one,' said Sidney. 'You can call yourself a marriage misguidance counsellor. We will also offer them the service of the agency's own private detective to collect any evidence of misconduct by the other half.'

'And what will my fee be for that?'

The voice came from one of the mail sacks that Sidney had carried up that morning. There was a rustling as from beneath the pile of letters sent in for the male nurse James Bedsop emerged.

'How long have you been there?' asked Sidney.

'You carried me up this morning,' said Bedsop. 'I was in the fourth sack.'

'No wonder I struggled,' said Sidney. 'Why couldn't you have got out and walked?'

'What, and blow my cover? No way. I pride myself on my ability to make myself virtually invisible. I have worked at being the Lon Chaney of private dicks.'

'Lon Chaney?' said Snooper.

'He was known in Hollywood as the "Man of A Thousand Faces",' explained Bedsop. 'They used to say

98

on any set of a film in which he was appearing, "Don't tread on that spider, it may be Lon Chaney".'

'So you've overheard everything we've discussed,' said Sidney.

'Well, no actually,' said Bedsop. 'You see I've lost so much sleep on my latest case that I nodded off.'

He looked suspiciously around the office to make sure there was nobody listening in. 'This is highly confidential and I would not tell a soul,' he said, now sitting cross-legged on the desk, 'but I have been hired by the Mayor to investigate his wife. He believes she's having him followed.'

'But it's you who's following him,' said Snooper.

'How do you know that?' said Bedsop, sharply. 'That's supposed to be confidential.'

'Because you told us.'

'Not me, sir. I take an oath of silence before every assignment. Anyway, and this is in strictest confidence, I shall be following the Mayor *and* the Mayoress.'

'But how can you follow them both?' said Sidney, knowing from experience that he had the greatest difficulty following just one person without making it obvious.

'I shall work double shifts,' said Bedsop. 'With my mastery of disguises and gift for not being seen, they will never know who I am or where I am.'

To prove his ability to make himself disappear from sight, Bedsop suddenly shouted at the door, 'Who's that? Go away!'

As Sidney and Snooper looked wide-eyed towards the door, Bedsop rolled himself in a ball and performed a rapid forward somersault and disappeared under the desk.

'Where the hell have you gone now?' said Sidney, giving a double take as he turned back to talk to a man who was no longer there.

'Try to find me,' Bedsop said, throwing his voice so that it seemed to come from the direction of the office window.

As Sidney and Snooper both looked towards the window, Bedsop scurried on all fours back to the mail sacks and crawled out of sight into the bag from which he had come.

Sidney was now opening the window to see if Bedsop was out on the ledge. Snooper was glancing all around the room. No sign of Bedsop.

'All right, James,' said Sidney. 'You've proved your point. Show yourself now and let's talk about the part you're going to play in the agency.'

Nothing.

'Stop mucking about,' said Snooper. 'Come out. We haven't got time for a game of hide 'n' seek.

Nothing.

In the sack, James Bedsop was fast asleep.

Sidney and Snooper were just about to start an inch-by-inch search of the office when the front door swung open and Bernie Biddle entered.

'I've just called in for the Phoebe Scratchitt details,' Bernie said. 'I would like you to fix me up with a date mate tonight, if possible.'

'We don't make dates anymore,' said Sidney. 'We only break them.'

100

'But you said you'd give me a free date with Phoebe Scratchitt,' Bernie protested. 'You've taken my ten pound deposit, and now you're going back on your word.'

'Oh all right,' Sidney said irritably. 'I'll phone Phoebe for you, but only in return for a favour.'

'What's that?' said Bernie.

'Take all these mailbags and throw them in your incinerator downstairs.'

'Okay,' said Bernie. 'I'll get it done while you're fixing me up with my date mate.'

Bernie picked up the sack containing the sleeping Bedsop. 'This is an 'eavy one,' he said. 'Do you want me to empty it first.'

'No,' said Sidney, getting Phoebe's card from the filing cabinet. 'It's just full of letters from shirt-lifters.'

As Bernie struggled down the stairs with the sack, Sidney telephoned Phoebe Scratchitt.

'Phoebe,' he said, 'this is Sidney Bliss.'

'Phoebe's not here,' Phoebe said. 'This is Fiona Feelit speaking.'

'Don't give me that nonsense, Phoebe. It's the agency. I *know* it's you.'

'And I'm telling you that this is Mary Muffit.'

'You see, Phoebe, you've used so many names that you've forgotten who you are.'

'Don't be ridiculous. This is Nora Nookie. What do you want?'

'I want to arrange a date for Phoebe Scratchitt,' Sidney said.

'She doesn't go out on dates any more. But I do. This

101

is Glenda Groper speaking.'

'Listen, Phoebe. I know you've had a lot of disappointments in the past and have a bit of a hang-up about being yourself, but the man I've lined up for you insists that he will only go out with the real Phoebe Scratchitt.'

'Just a minute,' said Phoebe, 'I'll put Phoebe on.'

There was a pause.

'Phoebe Scratchitt here. Who's this?'

'Sidney Bliss at the agency.'

'It's a long time since I've heard from you. Have you got me a date mate at last?'

'Yes, and he wants to take you out tonight.'

'What's he like?'

'Talk, dark and gruesome,' said Sidney, honestly.

'Sounds my type.'

'He's right up your street.'

'He lives in the same street as what I do?'

'It's just a figure of speech, Phoebe, but I promise you that you are perfectly matched. He wants to meet you in the saloon bar of the Pleasant Pheasant Plucker at eight o'clock.'

'What's the code word?'

'Uh, mailbag,' said Sidney off the top of his head.

'Right. I'll start getting myself ready now.'

While all this final date making was going on, Bernie was stoking up the incinerator at the back of the funeral parlour that was used for burning excess coffin wood, embalming remains and old clothes not needed by clients. He was about to toss the sack into the furnace when Bedsop woke up.

He poked his head out of the sack. 'Hello,' Bedsop said. 'I'm Lon Chaney.'

Bernie dropped the sack in terror and ran like the wind back upstairs. 'I nearly threw Lon Chaney in the incinerator,' he said as he burst into the office.

'Don't worry,' said Sidney. 'That wasn't Lon Chaney. That was a spider.'

'Blimey, it fooled me,' said Bernie. 'What a master of disguise.'

8

ANOTHER THREE thousand letters from fed-up husbands arrived the next morning, and now the first weakness in the scam became fairly evident as Sidney and Snooper sat staring at the mountains of envelopes surrounding them in the back office where they had both slept.

''ow do we reply to all these letters?' said Sidney. 'It's going to cost ten thousand threepenny stamps, plus another threepence for every envelope. How much is that?'

'In old money or new?' said Snooper, who was to Maths what Einstein was to ladies hairdressing. He scribbled numbers down on a piece of paper and mumbled away to himself while totting up columns of figures. 'Times six, carry three... multiplied by ten... got it. Six million pounds.'

'Don't be bloody stupid,' said Sidney. He got out a desk-top calculator, tapped away and then came up with the answer. 'It's six hundred quid, but it might as well be six million as far as I'm concerned. 'ow much money have you got in the bank?'

Snooper shrugged. 'Couldn't begin to tell you,' he said. 'Her Ladyship keeps all the accounts. I'm not even allowed a cheque book.'

Sidney's face clouded over with disappointment as he realised the logistics and financial barrier that he was facing before he could get his hands on the ten pound signing-on fees from all those hungry clients out there. 'I've just realised, for instance, that there's also the little matter of getting the undating ten commandments photocopied,' he said. 'They'll take up two pages each at fourpence a time. Then there's the printing costs for a minimum ten thousand sheets of agency headed notepaper...'

'And we'll have to get somebody in to type out all the envelopes,' said Snooper.

'What d'you mean, "get somebody in",' said Sidney. 'I can't afford to pay myself let alone a bleedin' typist. We'll have to type them ourselves.'

'Oooh, no,' said Snooper. 'Not me. I can't type. All that banging of keys gives me a headache, and my fingers are far too sensitive to be bashing away at a typewriter. You type, and I'll dictate.'

'But I can only type with two fingers,' said Sidney. 'It will take us days to do just a hundred envelopes. Even if you use just one of your delicate digits, you've got to help me type the envelopes.'

Snooper suddenly had a panic attack. 'We're d-o-o-m-e-d,' he whined. 'D-o-o-m-e-d I tell you. What are we going to do? I've walked out of my home and out of my job. Now we're stuck with ten thousand letters we can't reply to.'

'Shut up whining while I think,' said Sidney. 'There's got to be a way round this. Blimey, there's a potential hundred grand sitting in those letters just from enrolment fees alone.'

He placed his elbows on the desk and rested his crumpled face in the V-shape of his hands. After five minutes, he sat up straight with the gleam of hope back in his eyes. 'Got it,' he said. 'What we'll do is contact ten punters to start with. We can just about afford to post letters to them. Then, when their enrolment fees roll in, we shall select twenty more. Then another forty, and so on until we have contacted everybody, using the fees to bankroll us. It will become a self-financing business. What d'you think of that?'

Snooper was already on his hands and knees by the first pile pulling out ten letters at random.

Meanwhile, Sidney had a special assignment for James Bedsop. He found him in his filing cabinet, and instructed him to tail his wife. 'I want to know her every movement,' he said. 'She's seeing somebody and I need to know who he is and where he is.'

'Say no more, Mr Bliss,' said Bedsop, clambering out of the cabinet. 'This is a highly confidential matter just between the two of us. Now then, what's your wife's name and where does she live?'

'It's Sophie Bliss, of course,' said Sidney. 'You've worked for her on and off for the last five years.'

'How do you know that?' asked Bedsop with narrowed eyes. 'That is supposed to be a matter of confidentiality between me, my client and my conscience. Who ratted on me?'

'I used to give you a lift when you were following me, you idiot,' said Sidney.

'Ah, but that was before I got my masters degree at the Chameleon College of Disguise, which is in Hyde Park.'

'Hyde Park? I can't place it.'

'That's because it's camouflaged as a hot dog stall,' said Bedsop, arranging his face into a new shape. 'Can you guess who I look like?'

'No idea,' said Sidney.

Bedsop started hitching at his hips with the inside of his elbows. 'Now do you know?'

Sidney shrugged.

Bedsop changed his voice to an American accent. 'You dirty rat,' he said. 'One wrong move, and I'm going to blow your brains out.'

'Ah, President Nixon,' said Sidney.

'No, it's James Cagney,' said Bedsop, with a sulky look on his face. 'He played the part of Lon Chaney in the film *The Man with the Thousand Faces*.'

'How extremely interesting,' said Sidney. 'Now will you please put on one of your thousand faces and get on the trail of my wife. I want to know exactly what she's up to.'

As Bedsop climbed out of the office window and shinned down the drainpipe, Bernie Biddle came in the conventional way. For once in his life, his presence lit up the room and there was a glow coming from him that could have been measured in kilowatts.

'Gawd, who switched you on?' said Sidney.

'Phoebe Scratchitt, of course,' said Bernie. 'I've just come up to thank you for the introduction. She's the girl of my dreams.'

'She's the girl of most people's nightmares,' Sidney thought to himself. 'I knew you'd be right for each other,' he said. 'Where did you take her?'

'She took me actually,' said Bernie. 'We met in the

3Ps, and then after we'd both had a couple of pints of mild and bitter she talked me into going with her to the cemetery.'

'Don't tell me she's another necrophiliac,' said Sidney. 'That would be very grave news.'

'No, nothing like that,' said Bernie. 'She wanted to introduce me to her mother.'

'Her mother works at the cemetery?'

'No, she's buried there. Phoebe was keeping a promise to her to bring the first feller she really fancied to see her and just say hello.'

'Very romantic,' said Sidney. 'Cedric let you in, then.'

'Oh, didn't you know? Cedric's her father.'

'Phoebe's father? But she put down on her enrolment form that her old man was a professional violinist.'

'Well you should see the way he fiddles on that gate. He charged us a pound each to go in.'

'What, even his own daughter and her boyfriend?'

'Well, not really. It was just a deposit. He refunded the money when I brought her back. Said it was the only way he could guarantee her boyfriends bringing her back. I couldn't understand what he meant 'cos Phoebe told me that I was the first feller she'd ever taken to meet her mother.'

'I'm sure that's true,' said Sidney, knowing full well that all the dates she'd had with the agency had not wanted to get as far as her doorstep let alone her mother's graveside.

He shook Bernie's hand. 'Congratulations,' he said. 'I hope something comes of it.'

'Oh, didn't I tell you?' said Bernie. 'We're getting

married next month, and I want you to be my best man and Mrs Bliss to be Phoebe's matron of honour.'

'Uh, well we'll see about that,' said Sidney. 'To be honest I've switched sides. I'm now more into divorce than marriage. Breaking 'em rather than making 'em. Your marriage fee will be the last that I collect.'

From the back office came a cry of triumph. 'I've just finished typing the first envelope,' shouted Snooper, the one-finger terror of the typewriter keys. It had taken him three hours.

Sophie Bliss had just completed chapter five of her novel. This dealt with murder by drowning, and she had lured ~~Sidney~~ Rodney into accepting a round-the-world rowing race challenge from Chay Blyth, and had great entertainment writing about how his sabotaged boat, full of leaking holes that she had drilled into the bottom, overturned under Tower Bridge right at the start of the race. As he was going under for the third time he was gobbled up by a killer shark. She made a mental note to double check whether any killer sharks had ever been known to actually get as far as the Tower. If not, she would have him slowly strangled by a wriggle of killer eels.

James Bedsop, disguised as a dining room chair, watched over her shoulder and made notes.

Sophie had a strange feeling that she was being followed when she went first to the local shops for her groceries and then to the bank to draw out every single penny that the agency overdraft allowed before Sidney thought of it. She looked over her shoulder several times, but all she could see was first an old tramp, then a parking meter – for some reason in the middle of the pavement – and, with the third backward glance, a clown juggling with his balls. 'Now there's a novelty,' thought Sophie in the best traditions of Eric Morecambe.

She was into her fourth day of freedom from Sidney, and the tears and fears of the first night had now given way to a grim determination to make the most of her time alone and away from his moans and groans and continual grumbles about the problems of the dating agency business. She felt as if a black cloud of despondency had been lifted off her, and she decided that what she needed in her life was a little sunshine. The thought just happened to coincide with her passing by the high street travel agency. On the spur of the moment she turned back, almost colliding with a children's nanny pushing a pram. She apologised to the nanny for getting in her way and smiled into the pram. To her surprise it contained not a baby but a briefcase.

Thinking no more of it, she walked into the travel agency and sat down at the first desk. A name slide on the desk made her quietly smile to herself: RODNEY TWISTLETHWAITE. The agent spotted the smile as he sat down facing her. 'Yeth,' he said, with a waterspray of a lisp, 'my name is alwayth good for a thmile. Thath's thwhy I never think of changing it. Ith's a great ithe breaker. "My name'th Twithlethwaite," I thay to complete thrangerth in the pub. "What'th yourth?" They alwaysth thay 'mine'th a pint,' and an inthant friendthip ith forged.'

110

Sophie noticed the limpness of his wrist and the pout of the lips, and guessed just what sort of friendship he was talking about.

'Actually I was smiling at Rodney,' she said.

'Thurely that'th not thuch a thrange name,' said Twistlethwaite. 'I mean there have been lotth of famouth Rodneyth. Laver, the tennith player. Marth, the footballer. Oh, don't you juth love his thighth?'

'No, it's just that I have become very attached to a man named Sidney, sorry, cross that out, I mean Rodney.'

'How very nith. Now what can I do for you?'

'Not a lot,' Sophie thought, blushing. 'I was wondering,' she said aloud, 'about a holiday, somewhere in the sun. Not too expensive, but nice and warm.'

'Not too expenthive, but nith and warm,' repeated Twistlethwaite. 'Now let me thee. How about Nicth in the Thouth of Franth. That'sth nithe at thith time of the year.'

'But isn't it very pricey down there?'

'Not if you thtay in a caravan or a tent,' he said. 'Alternatively, you can go to the Cothta del Thol. Theven nightth for jutht theventy-theven poundth.'

'Oh, no, that's a bit too expensive for me, I'm afraid,' said Sophie. 'What have you got for about the fifty pounds mark.'

'How about a long weekend in Parith?'

'That sounds wonderful,' said Sophie, with warm, distant memories of her honeymoon there. 'How about the weekend after next?'

111

Bedsop had just arrived and he crouched alongside the desk disguised as a potted plant, making a note as Twistlethwaite took a ten pound deposit and confirmed the booking.

Sophie again had the strange feeling that she was being followed as she left the travel agency. She stopped and pretended to look in a shoe shop window but instead studied the reflection as she had seen Orson Welles do in *The Third Man*. A James Cagney lookalike was walking by in a belted macintosh that she would recognise anywhere. She followed on behind, hopping in and out of doorways as he kept looking around for his quarry. He had not seen her stop at the shop window because he had been busy switching disguises.

As he prepared to go into the undertaker's to give a report to Sidney, Sophie caught up with him. 'Good morning, Mr Bedsop,' she called.

He was completely taken by surprise. 'Oh, uh, good morning, Mrs Bliss,' he said, trying not to look as flustered as he felt. 'Nice time for the weather of the year we're having.'

'I want a word with you,' she said, beckoning him to follow her.

She led him round the corner to where her Mini was parked. 'Right, get in,' she ordered. He sat in the passenger seat, and she got in behind the wheel.

'What sort of loyalty is this?' she said. 'All the work I've given you over the past five years, and you repay me by snooping on me.'

'I've not been snooping,' Bedsop said, his hands wrestling nervously in his lap. 'I cannot tell you just

112

what I'm up to because it is a matter of complete confidentially between me and my client, but I've been following you on your husband's orders.'

'Oh, really,' Sophie said. 'And just what is the worm up to?'

'I couldn't possibly divulge that, ma'am,' said Bedsop, 'but it's to do with the new agency we're starting together.'

'*You're* starting together,' said Sophie. 'What do you mean, *you're* starting together?'

'I have been sworn to secrecy, and all I can tell you is that it is called The Undating Agency...'

'The *Undating* agency?' said Sophie, failing to stop a look of disbelief engulfing her features. 'What on earth is that?'

'Well, and this is in strictest confidence of course, it's like a dating agency but it breaks up couples instead of bringing them together.'

'I see,' said Sophie, not really seeing at all. 'And who else is involved in this little scam... scheme, I mean, apart from you and my husband?'

'Sorry, ma'am, but my lips are sealed. You could apply pliers to my tongue but I would still not reveal that it's the marriage guidance counsellor Percival Snooper. I wouldn't tell you this either, ma'am, but they're in the office now preparing to send out the agency's ten commandments to their first members.'

Sophie took a five pound note from her purse. 'I admire your loyalty to your client and appreciate the way you need to keep their confidence,' she said. 'Now here's a fiver. I want you to smuggle me out a copy of

113

their ten commandments and deliver it to me at my house by no later than tea-time. All right?'

'All right, ma'am,' said Bedsop, throwing a salute. 'It's nice to be working for you again, and you can trust me to keep everything in absolute confidence.'

Sophie let him out, and then drove off in the direction of the home of the Snoopers. She had a lot to talk about to Mrs Patsy Snooper, who she personally had lined up as Percival's wife when they were clients of the Wedded Bliss Matrimonial Dating Agency.

Bedsop pulled a famous face from his gallery so that nobody would recognise him leaving the car, and headed back to the office to make his confidential report.

Sidney had just finished typing the ten commandments ready to be photocopied and Snooper was in the back office tapping out his fifth envelope when they were interrupted by a knock at the door.

For security reasons, the door was now locked and Sidney was astonished when he opened it to find Opposition Leader Harold Wilson standing there sucking on his pipe.

'Blimey, don't tell me you're a fed-up husband,' he said. 'I suppose Mary's driving you mad with all her poems.'

'It's me, Bedsop. James Bedsop, private dick.'

Sidney sat Bedsop on the chair in front of his desk, and then sat down on his lap to make sure that he could not disappear again.

'Right,' said Sidney, 'give me a full report. What's my

114

wife been up to?'

'I'm afraid it's not the sort of news you'll want to hear, Mr Bliss,' said Bedsop. 'In fact it's not the sort of thing anybody would want to hear.'

'Just give it to me straight,' said Sidney, bracing himself.

'She's planning to murder you.'

Sidney's face, already looking as worn as an old wallet, ran the full gamut of expressions from shock, through astonishment, incredulity, fear, disbelief and back to shock. 'She's planning to do what?' he said, forcing the words out through a mouth suddenly short of breath.

'She's planning to murder you,' Bedsop repeated as matter-of-factly as if reporting a car-parking problem.

'What do you mean she's planning to murder me?'

'I'm only telling you what I found out by careful and diligent detective work,' said Bedsop. 'I tricked my way into your house by pretending to be next door's cat, and then sat alongside her disguised as a dining room chair. I saw her draw up a list of possible ways to murder you.'

'A list?' said Sidney. 'She's planning more than one way to murder me?'

'From what I could see of her typed notes, she is considering one of five methods: strangulation, poisoning, murder by accident, drowning, and putting a contract out on you.'

'But why? Why does she want to murder me? I can understand her wanting a separation or a divorce. But murder? Somebody else must be putting her up to it.'

115

'Correct,' said Bedsop.

'You know who it is?'

Bedsop nodded 'It's Mr Twistlethwaite.'

'Who the bleedin' hell is Mr Twistlethwaite?'

'He works in the high street travel agency,' said Bedsop. 'He's taking your wife to Paris the weekend after next.'

'Are you sure? She's going to Paris with a geezer called Twistelthwaite.'

'That's right. He's got his name on his desk. Rodney Twis...'

'Rodney,' roared Sidney, getting off Bedsop's lap and stalking the office like a wounded tiger. 'Rodney. That's the geezer. Well Rodney bleedin' Twistlethwaite is going to thwish he wasn't born.'

While Sidney was planning an assault and battery on Rodney and a defence against the murder plots of his wife, he sent Bedsop to get ten photocopies of the ten commandments.

The detective adopted his two-faced disguise, and had eleven copies run off.

9

IT WAS JUST Sidney's luck that Rodney Twistlethwaite had been the victim of a mugging eighteen months earlier. Since then he had taken lessons in self defence, and had become a master of the martial arts and always carried a samurai sword hidden inside a cello case. So he was more than well prepared to defend himself when a raging maniac accosted him as he was leaving the travel agency to keep an evening appointment with his music teacher.

'Oi, you mush,' said a dangerously out of control Sidney, standing directly in the path of Twistlethwaite after he had locked the door to the high street shop. 'Planned any good murders lately?'

'Are you talking to me, thur?' lisped Rodney.

'You're Rodney Twistlethwaite,' said Sidney, more as a statement of fact than a question.

'Yeth, that'th me.'

'Right, put down that fiddle and prepare for the hiding of your life,' said Sidney, who might have done well during a short professional boxing career had the referee not kept treading on his hands. He had been nicknamed the Rembrandt of the Ring because he spent so much time on the canvas. Nevertheless, he had still been useful with his fists and knew he could flatten the flouncey fool in front of him. No problem.

'I muth warn you, thur,' said Rodney, 'that my hanth are dangerouth weaponth, and if you perthitht in

117

making a nuisanth of yourthelf I shall be forthed to take action for which I thall not be held rethponthible.'

'That old trick,' thought Sidney with a grim smile. 'Next he'll be saying he's not got a fiddle but a sword in his case.'

'Listen, sunshine,' he growled. 'I'm telling you one more time. Put that fiddle down and put your hands up. I'm going to book you for a hospital rather than a holiday.'

Rodney decided to try to pacify him. 'Look, thur,' he said, 'if one of our holidayth did not come up to expectationth I am prepared to conthider a refund. But violenth is not the anther.'

An enraged Sidney knocked the cello case out of his hands. 'Look, I know you've been plotting with my wife to get rid of me,' he said. 'Well now you're going to pay for it in spades.'

'Wife?... thpadth?' said Rodney, who had dropped into a crouch taught to him by the chief *sensei* of the ancient school of karate in Shikoku. 'I don't know what you're talking about, but I give you a final warning that my hanth are lethal weaponth.'

Words had deserted Sidney. It was now time for decisive action. He got up on to the balls of his feet and threw the good old traditional one-two, a left jab followed by a powerful right cross. Both punches made contact only with thin air, and Sidney was suddenly surprised at the immense size of Rodney Twistlethwaite. He was much taller than he thought.

Sidney then realised that he was looking up at him from the floor.

Rodney had delivered a lightning *Yoko-gerikeomi* with his right foot, which if Sidney had been in a more receptive mood would have been explained to him as a side thrust kick launched from the waist. The Rembrandt of the Ring was reduced to the Picasso of the Pavement.

Sidney hauled himself up, as he had countless times before – correction, counted-over times before – and rushed at Rodney with his head down, Marciano-style and throwing a blur of hooking punches.

Rodney stood his ground and unleashed a pulverising *mawashi-geri* to the temple, which for the layman – as Sidney now was, because he was lying flat out – is a high and exceedingly powerful roundhouse kick.

The kick had knocked Sidney cold, and as he came out of his brief concussive state he saw through blurred eyes that his assailant was opening his fiddle case. The thought flashed through his mind that the maniac was about to serenade him. He should be so lucky.

There was a glint of steel, and it came through to Sidney's dulled brain at one mile an hour that it was not a Stradivarius being raised above Rodney's head but some kind of curved sword. The *mawashi-geri* blow had not only parted Sidney from his senses, but had also numbed his nerves and his limbs would not obey his command to get the hell out of there.

Rodney released a blood-curdling ancient Japanese war cry. Sidney considered that his last thought before departing this mortal coil was going to be that he had discovered to whom Sophie had given the murder contract. She had obviously decided on decapitation.

119

An execution most foul.

There was a blur of flashing steel as Rodney chopped away at the mad man who had been insane enough to accuse him of plotting with his wife. There was not a wife on this earth, or any woman for that matter, with whom he would have had any sort of dealings, and certainly not of the plotting variety.

He exhausted himself flailing away with the sword, and did not stop until he had divested his victim of just about every inch of a ghastly Prince of Wales checked suit for which he should have been murdered for showing such awful taste.

Then he calmly returned the sword to the cello case, looked down at the cut-up figure of Sidney and said: 'Let that be a lethon to you.' He then continued on his way, leaving Sidney lying in a pool of sweat and very little else.

Sidney, surrounded by the remnants of his suit, had to bite his bottom lip to stop himself from crying. He did not even have the satisfaction of being able to claim that he had been leading on points.

Percival Snooper was having enormous difficulty remembering that he was now a marriage misguidance counsellor.

Facing him across the desk was Gerald Chilblain, a middle-aged client that he had found wandering in a tearful daze at the foot of the stairs. 'I've come about my wife,' he had said, 'She never understood me from the first day of our marriage.'

Snooper invited him upstairs and was now doing his

best to advise him. 'Why do you feel she never understood you?' he asked.

'Mainly because she was German,' he said, 'and couldn't speak a word of English.'

'Yes, well that would put a strain on any marriage,' admitted Snooper. 'When did you get married?'

'The week before last,' Chilblain said.

'Well really,' said Snooper, wearing the wrong hat. 'You haven't given it a chance, have you? It would take any normal couple months, maybe even years to understand each other, but with your wife being a foreigner in a strange land, well you would need extra special patience.'

'This is not the sort of thing I expected to be hearing from you,' said Chilblain, dabbing at his tearful eyes with a handkerchief.

'Oh, I'm sorry,' said a horrified Snooper. 'Do forgive me. Force of habit. What you should have done right from day one is tell her that she's an old German bag and that she should get back to sauerkraut land where she belongs.'

Chilblain dropped his head down on to the desk and started to sob.

'Come on, Mr Chilblain,' pleaded Snooper. 'It could be worse. You've got us to help you now. We'll put a tail on her and find out who she is having leg-over relationships with.'

Chilblain looked up from the desk with a look of disbelief and disgust on his face. 'How can you say these things?' he said. 'You're talking about the only woman I've ever loved.'

121

'So why come here?' said Snooper, losing his patience. 'All we can do is help you get rid of her.'

As Chilblain started to break into more sobs, there was a sharp double knock at the door. Snooper opened it to find Ivor Bodie standing on the landing in an even blacker mood than usual.

He pushed his way in and stared at Chilblain. 'Are you Mr Chilblain by any chance?' he asked.

Chilblain nodded.

'What are you doing with my client?' Bodie said, snarling at Snooper.

'Your client?' said Snooper. 'But I found him downstairs crying because his wife didn't understand him.'

'That's quite right,' said Bodie. 'He was shouting at her to "watch out for that bus" but she didn't understand him and got run over. I had invited him to my funeral parlour to discuss burial arrangements.'

They were interrupted by the arrival of Sidney, who was wearing a two-sizes-too-big flare-bottomed suit that he had borrowed from George Drinkwater at the Pleasant Pheasant Plucker.

Bodie steered Chilblain out of the office, giving Sidney a look of contempt. 'Come on, Mr Chilblain,' he said. 'Let me take you away from these hippies.'

'What are you doing in that clown's suit?' said Snooper.

'Well it's a long story,' said Sidney, 'but let me just summarise it by saying that I was attacked by a Japanese warrior in the high street who had a sword in a fiddle case. I think my wife has either put out a

122

contract on me or, just possibly, our private detective might have got mixed up. And if he has, I shall take a sword to his private dick.'

'I see,' said an open-mouthed Snooper, silently wondering to himself if it was too late to get back his lovely old straightforward, uncomplicated job as a marriage guidance counsellor.

It was with a bewilderment bordering on astonishment that Sophie Bliss opened her front door to find a coal man standing there with a sack of coal on his shoulders. 'Where d'you want this, lady?' he said, pushing his way into the hall.

'But I don't want any coal,' she protested.

It was too late as one hundred weight of best nutty slack was tipped on to the kitchen floor.

'You silly man,' Sophie said, stamping her foot. 'This must be meant for next door.'

Suddenly she realised she was not talking to a coal man, but to Bedsop.

'Sorry about the entrance, ma'am,' he said, 'but I did not want to raise any suspicions with the neighbours.'

'Well you'll have them talking their heads off,' said Sophie. 'They all know we've got central heating.'

They were joined in the kitchen by Patsy Snooper. 'What's going on?' she said. 'Why's there a mountain of coal here? You've got central heating, haven't you?'

Bedsop tensed. This one asked too many questions. He feared his cover was about to be blown.

Sophie glared at Bedsop. 'Patsy Snooper, meet private detective Bedsop.'

'I would appreciate it if you would keep my identity to yourself, ma'am,' said Bedsop, blackening Patsy's hand as he shook it. 'I'm here at great risk and on a matter of complete confidentiality about The Undating Agency run by your husbands.'

'Did you get a copy of the commandments?' Sophie asked.

Bedsop reached down into the coal sack and brought out two sheets of black paper.

'How are we supposed to be able to read this?' said Sophie.

Bedsop blew the thick layer of coal dust off the paper, and a cloud of it settled on Sophie and Patsy.

'You can just about read it now, ma'am,' said Bedsop. 'I had to keep it tucked out of the way in case I was stopped and searched.'

'Why on earth would anybody stop and search a coal man?' said Sophie, quickly wishing she had never asked.

'You never know with today's alert young bobbies,' said Bedsop. 'They might think it suspicious me getting off a bus with a hundred weight of coal on my back.'

'You came by bus?' said Patsy. 'You haven't got a coal lorry?'

More questions. Bedsop sensed he had to be wary of this one.

'Why d'you want to know, ma'am?' he asked.

'It just seems a teeny-weeny bit odd that you should come by bus when you're disguised as a coal man,' said Patsy.

Bedsop's mind was racing. Could she, he wondered, be in cahoots with the bus conductor? He had asked similar probing questions. He decided he would test her.

'Have you had your ticket clipped lately, lady?' he asked in his best Bogart voice.

'I beg your pardon?' said Patsy.

Bedsop sensed that he had already got her rattled. 'Can't beat the old 69, can you?' he said.

Patsy's response was electrifying. The open palm of her right hand slapped across his face at the speed of light, and his left cheek looked zebra-like where her fingers had left stripes in the coal dust.

Bedsop guessed he had stumbled on to a code. The 69 bus route was obviously the key to whatever conspiracy she was involved in.

Sophie led a weeping Patsy towards the lounge. 'Get this coal cleared up and out of the house,' she commanded over her shoulder. 'Then come and see me. I've got another assignment for you.'

She gave Patsy her fourth glass of medicinal brandy, hoping to stop her continually breaking into tears at any mention of her husband, marriage or anything remotely connected with matters sexual.

'You've got to pull yourself together, Patsy,' she said. 'Ignore Bedsop. He was just talking his usual poppycock.'

More tears.

'But I want him back,' she sobbed. 'He's not much, but he is mine.'

'I know, I know,' said Sophie, trying to comfort her by being as sympathetic and understanding as possible. 'I'd feel the same in your position. This whole business has obviously brought you to your knees.'

More tears.

More brandy.

A lot more tears were shed as Sophie read the commandments out aloud. When it came to the instruction about barring the mother-in-law, Sophie joined in the bawling.

'What's my mother ever done wrong to him?' she asked nobody in particular. 'All right, so she does nag him when he's driving, and she has been known to make him sit outside her house when his shoes have been dirty, and she did once hit him on the head with the frying pan when he came home late from the pub, and there was that one time when she tethered his testicles to his boot laces when he fell into a drunken sleep on her sofa, but she always means well.'

More brandy. This time for Sophie.

By the time they had finished off the bottle between them, Sophie and Patsy were prepared for all-out war. They drew the battle lines on the back of chapter six of *Ten Ways to Murder Your Husband:* Burn the Bastard.

Bedsop had reappeared in the lounge disguised as Al Jolson. It meant that he did not have to bother to scrub off all the coal dust.

'Right Bedshop,' slurred Sophie, 'come and shit here on the shofa with Shophie while I show you shomething quite shtartling.'

She patted the sofa to indicate that Bedsop should join her. 'No, thank you mammy,' said Bedsop, worried about what web he was about to be drawn into. 'Sonny boy does not want to climb upon your knee. I just want my instructions so that I can complete my assignment, get paid and then get on with the next job, mammy.'

'Pleashe yourshelf,' said Sophie. 'I wash jusht going to show you the advertishment that we want you to placshe for ush in the *Advertisher*.'

Bedsop took the scribbled sheets of paper, glanced at them and slipped them inside one of his white gloves.

'I need the money to pay for it, mammy,' he said, beginning to feel uncomfortable on one knee with his arms stretched wide.

'Don't worry Shonny boy,' said a suddenly beaming Patsy. 'You take me up to bed and I'll pay you all the money you want.'

'I'd normally walk a million miles for one of your smiles,' said Bedsop diplomatically.

'But you ain't sheen nothing yet,' said Patsy, dipsomaniacally.

'Unfortunately I have to say goodbye, Tootsie,' said Bedsop, getting off his knee. 'The last 69 bus leaves in five minutes.'

Neighbours still clucking about the coal man's visit had a whole new bookful of gossip when they saw Sophie and Patsy following a man dressed as Al Jolson down the garden path singing, 'Swanee, how I love ya, how I love ya, my dear old Swanee...'

The conductor on his return journey on route 69 shook his head in disbelief when Al Jolson asked him for a one-way ticket to California's Golden Gate where the flowers, the flowers they bloom in the spring.

'You wouldn't believe the nuts we get on here, Al pal,' he said. 'We had a coal man on earlier who insisted on sitting downstairs 'cos he said the sack on his back contained "no smoking" fuel.'

The journey to the high street was one of the most enjoyable the conductor could ever remember, with the entire bus joining in the choruses of 'April Showers' and 'Toot Toot Tootsie Goodbye'.

When he got off the bus, Bedsop had two pounds in coins collected from the passengers and he briefly wondered if there was money to be made out of a stage show featuring Jolson. But no, he decided, that would never work. Who would go and see an Englishman blacked up as Jolson?

As he turned into the *Advertiser* office Bedsop changed his expression and his body posture and arrived at the advertising counter as Kenny Lynch.*

'I wish to place an advert, please luv,' he said to the male supervisor.

He read through it, and then called over his married female assistant.

'I think you had better deal with this,' he said. 'I think it's quite revolting.'

Kenny Lynch paid for the advertisement, and then walked to the lift. 'If you want me,' he said, 'I'll be up on the roof.'

The supervisor shook his head as he watched him go into the lift. 'Don't worry,' he said. 'It's only nutty Bedsop on the loose again. He couldn't detect a smell in a sewer.'

Carry On aficionados will know that Kenny Lynch featured in the film version of *Carry On Loving* as a bus conductor.

10

```
━━━━━━ ATTENTION ALL FED-UP WIVES ━━━━━━
DO YOU WANT HELP GETTING OUT OF THE TANGLED
   WEB YOU WEAVED WHEN YOU MADE THE FATAL
 MISTAKE OF GETTING MARRIED? WE CAN SHOW YOU
   THE WAY TO FREEDOM AND THE ROAD BACK TO
   HAPPINESS. WRITE NOW FOR YOUR COPY OF TEN
 WAYS TO MURDER YOUR HUSBAND. SEND A STAMPED
   ADDRESSED ENVELOPE FOR FULL DETAILS TO...
━━━━━━ BURN THE BASTARD BOX 999 ━━━━━━
```

SOPHIE, suffering a hangover that she would not have
wished on anybody but Sidney, could not believe
what she was reading as she studied the advertisement
placed in the *Advertiser*. Ten Ways to Murder Your
Husband and Burn the Bastard had been on the reverse
side of the advertising copy. How on earth had it
become mixed up with an invitation to join an undating
agency for wives? She would never ever again trust that
dopey man Bedsop with anything.

The damage had been done now, and she would just
have to wait and see what the response would be. 'It's
no good crying over spilt newspaper ink,' she said to
Patsy, who was still in the mood to cry over just about
anything.

They were sitting together in the lounge of the Bliss
home thinking up their own ten commandments to
counter the list compiled by their husbands. Patsy, who
had previously only ever drunk Communion wine, had

an icepack on her forehead, and a handkerchief in her hand to wipe the tears.

'Why is Percival being so cruel to me?' she whimpered. 'I've only treated him the way mummy said I should. On the eve of our getting married, mummy said to me, "Marriage is all about inches – the six that you want from him in bed and the one that you will never trust him." So I've never trusted Percival an inch since.'

'What about the, uh, six inches?' asked Sophie, just for curiosity's sake.

'Oh, yes, we always manage to keep at least six inches apart in bed,' she said. 'He's been very good that way. Percival is a proper gentleman in bed and has never ever taken a liberty with me.'

'You mean that you've never, um, well... you know, consummated it...?'

'Oh no, Percival, doesn't like consommé soup,' Patsy said. 'He much prefers tomato, and occasionally he has minestrone.'

'That's not quite what I meant,' said Sophie. 'I mean don't you ever, you know... uh, play Miss Pussy and the Postman?'

'Oh goodness me, no. Percival is allergic to cats. Comes out in a rash, poor thing. And the postman has no interest in games whatsoever, apart from postman's knock I suppose.'

Sophie was near to exhaustion. She decided to go down the Sidney road. 'But don't you ever do IT?' she said.

'What?' said Patsy. 'You mean sex? Oh goodness, yes.

All the time. That's what's wrong with our marriage. We can't leave each other alone.'

Deflated, Sophie retreated back to the main item on their agenda; in fact the only item. The ten commandments for wives who want to change their lives.

'I think we should be more subtle than the men,' she said. 'What we have to do is come up with ten commandments that really torture the husbands and make them realise that they are out of their depth taking us on.'

'You mean things like put salt on their cornflakes and starch in their underpants?' said Patsy. 'But I already do that.'

'Well, no, not exactly,' said Sophie. 'I was thinking that we could be just a wee bit more wicked.'

Working her imagination hard, Sophie – hindered rather than helped by the tearful Patsy – came up with the following commandments for fed-up wives wanting to break away from their husbands:

TEN COMMANDMENTS FOR WIVES
WHO WANT NEW LIVES

1. THOU SHALT PLEDGE TO MAKE YOUR HUSBAND'S LIFE A MISERY UNTIL HE BEGS FOR THE MARRIAGE TO BE OVER.
2. THOU SHALT COVET THY NEIGHBOUR'S HUSBAND OR ANYBODY ELSE'S HUSBAND IF THE MOOD TAKES YOU.
3. THOU SHALT RESOLUTELY REFUSE TO WASH ANOTHER DISH OR SWEEP ANOTHER FLOOR UNLESS YOUR HUSBAND AGREES TO TAKE AN EQUAL SHARE OF THE WORKLOAD.

131

4. THOU SHALT CUT UP EACH OF HIS SUITS INTO TINY SQUARES IF YOU CATCH HIM HAVING A BIT ON THE SIDE.
5. THOU SHALT THEN LET DOWN THE TYRES ON HIS CAR AND PUT SAND IN HIS PETROL TANK.
6. THOU SHALT HAVE HIS GOLF CLUBS SAWN UP AND PLACED ON A BLAZING FIRE.
7. THOU SHALT FIX HIS TESTICLES TO THE DOG LEAD WHILE HE IS ASLEEP AND THEN SHOUT 'WALKIES'.
8. THOU SHALT GO SHOPPING WITH HIS CREDIT CARD AND TAKE HIM FOR EVERY PENNY HE'S GOT.
9. THOU SHALT INSIST THAT HE CUTS THE GRASS AFTER YOU HAVE LAID THE LAWN WITH LAND MINES.
10. THOU SHALT REFUSE HIM NOOKIE, NO MATTER HOW MUCH HE GETS DOWN ON HIS KNEES AND BEGS FOR IT.

It was Patsy who suggested that commandment number nine was a little bit over the top. 'After all,' she said, 'think of the dear little worms, robins and beetles that could be blown up.'

'True,' said Sophie. 'Let's make it that they have to cut the grass while listening to Jimmy Osmond sing.'

'Ouch, wicked,' said Patsy. 'Perhaps we should stick with the land mines.'

They were interrupted by the ringing of the telephone.

'Hello, Sophie Bliss speaking.'

'Can I speak to Mrs Sophie Bliss please?'

'Sophie Bliss speaking.'

'Oh, hello. Are you Sophie Bliss?'

'Speaking.'

'Ah, I was given your telephone number by the

Evening Advertiser. You are Mrs Sophie Bliss?'

'Do you want me to push my passport down the telephone? For goodness sake, yes I AM Mrs Sophie Bliss. Who are you?'

'Ah, so nice to speak to you Mrs Bliss. My name is Sir Rodney Woodman, and I am the managing director of the Andrew Belgique publishing company. I was very intrigued by your advertisement in this evening's *Advertiser*.'

'Sorry, but we deal with fed-up wives only,' said Sophie, and put down the telephone.

Two minutes later the telephone rang again.

'Hello, Sophie Bliss speaking.'

'Is this Mrs Sophie Bliss?'

'Don't let's go through all that again. I've already told you, we are dealing with fed-up wives only.'

'But I'm only interested in your book.'

'Which book?'

'*Ten Ways to Murder Your Husband*, volume one: Burn the Bastard.'

'That's not a volume, that's a chapter.'

'I see, and how many chapters are there?'

'Would you believe ten?'

'Yes, that would make sense. Now then, do you have a publisher?'

'Not yet. I'm only just over halfway through writing the book.'

'Well I would be very interested in seeing the manuscript with a view to publishing it. It sounds a fascinating subject.'

It suddenly clicked with Sophie.

133

'Bedsop, you idiot. Get off the line.'

Bedsop, listening in on headphones in his role as a secret bugger, froze with fear.

'Do we have a crossed line?' asked Sir Rodney.

'Listen,' Sophie hissed into the mouthpiece, 'you little piece of slime. You almost fooled me with the coal man and your Al Jolson was very believable, but it's just a waste of time impersonating an anonymous publisher on the telephone.' She slammed down the receiver.

Two minutes later, the telephone rang again.

'Hello, Sophie Bliss speaking.'

'I am who I am, Mrs Bliss, I promise you. Please don't hang up again until I have had time to make a suggestion.'

'If it's a rude one, you can stay on the line as long as you like. That's a joke by the way.'

'Yes, very witty Mrs Bliss. What I would like to suggest is that I come to see you and have a read through what you have written so far. If it is as commercially viable as I believe it could be, then I would be prepared to offer you a contract and a cash advance to give you that extra incentive.'

'You have just spoken my language, Sir Rodney. Cashlish. Please call this evening at seven, and I will show you the first six chapters. I am about to start on chapter seven: Murder by Sex.'

'My goodness. How does that work?'

'You simply keep making demands on them in bed. All the time, non-stop. You exhaust them every night and every morning.'

'But don't you run the risk of killing yourself?'

'True, but what a lovely way to go.'

'Quite, Mrs Bliss. Until this evening then.'

'All right, Sir Rodney. I look forward to seeing you.'

Sir Rodney replaced his receiver. Sophie put her telephone down.

Bedsop, private dick, took off his earphones and returned to his cover of repairing a hole in the road outside the Bliss house. It had taken him three-and-a-half hours earlier that morning to make the hole in his guise as a council worker armed with a pneumatic drill. Nobody had ever explained to him that those things were supposed to be plugged in to an electric point, and it had nearly worn him out digging a hole deep enough for him to hide in while tapping into Mrs Bliss's telephone calls.

Sidney gaped as he sat in his office reading the fed-up wives advertisement in the *Advertiser*, which Bedsop had warned him about in strictest confidence. Sophie was not only hell bent on murdering him, but also getting all wives in on the killing fields.

He knew Sophie well enough – well, he thought he did – to know that she would not have dreamed up such an evil scheme by herself. And she certainly would not have had the business sense to ask for stamped addressed envelopes to be included (he just wish he had thought of that).

Sophie had, Sidney decided, obviously come under the mesmerising influence of some Japanese warrior sect, and that sword-swishing maniac Rodney Twistlethwaite was clearly her Svengali. He was

135

convinced there was nothing sexual between them. Blimey, he looked effeminate enough to be the fairy godmother.

Who else, Sidney wondered, could possibly have been behind this mass-murder plot? He had a sudden suspicion.

'How well d'you know your wife?' he asked out of the blue, making Percival Snooper jump as he concentrated with furrowed brow on looking for the 'F' on the typewriter keyboard. He was halfway through the tenth envelope.

'What do you mean how well do I know her?'

'Do you really know her background?' Sidney asked. 'Where she comes from, where she was educated, where she grew up, who her friends were, her major influences while she was growing up. That sort of thing. What do you really know about your wife?'

'Only that rubbish your computer allegedly fed us when we were first dating,' said Snooper. 'Why do you ask?'

'I just wondered if you knew whether she had any connections with Japan?'

'Japan? That's a funny question, but since you ask she does go to evening classes to study origami.'

'Ah, ah,' said Sidney, his suspicions strengthening. 'How long has this been going on?'

'Well she signed on after reading an advert in which she thought it said "teach yourself orgasms" but she decided to stick with it when she found it was actually origami. It probably explains why she breathes heavily every time she folds a bit of paper.'

136

A likely story, Sidney thought.

'Does she happen to have had anything to do with a chap called Twistlethwaite?' he asked. 'Rodney Twistlethwaite?'

'You mean that chap who turned your suit into chop suey? She did book a holiday through him once. Seven days in Bognor.'

'Aha,' said Sidney. 'The plot thickens.'

'What plot?' said Snooper. 'I do wish you'd stop talking double Dutch.'

'It's not the Dutch I'm worried about,' said Sidney. 'It's those Orientals I'm concerned about. They've brain washed my wife, and I wouldn't be surprised if your missus is involved in it all as well.'

Snooper sat staring into space.

'It's funny,' he said, coming back from what had been a world of his own, 'but she has been acting oddly lately. She's been doing Yoga...'

'That's not Japanese.'

'No, but it's near enough. And she's also been eating lots of raw fish.'

'Aha,' said Sidney. 'That certainly points the finger. Anything else?'

'She said how much better the first half was of the film *Tora! Tora! Tora!* which was all in Japanese and which we saw together last year. She wanted to leave once Pearl Harbor had been bombed.'

Sidney puffed out his cheeks. 'Wow, anything else to connect her with the Japanese?'

Snooper concentrated hard. 'I recall that she cried all the way through *Sayonara*,' he said. 'Mind you, I have to admit that I cried too when Marlon Brando's girlfriend died.'

'This is getting serious,' said Sidney.

'She's always singing songs from *Madame Butterfly* and *The Mikado*,' said Snooper, 'and when we had a choice between a Sony or a Ferguson television set last month she chose the Sony.'

'That's the clincher,' said Sidney. 'I'm afraid all the evidence points to the fact that you've married a Japanese mole.'

'Well don't blame me,' spat Snooper, slipping into the grip of another panic attack. 'It was your rotten agency that put us together. I was quite happy minding my own business in the marriage guidance office, and then suddenly, poof, you conned me into dating her and mating her. God, what have you done to me? What's going to become of me? My job, my wife, my home. Everything has gone. I am d-o-o-m-e-d. D-o-o-m-e-d, I tell you.'

Sidney was too deep into plot unravelling to concern himself with Snooper's despair and anguish. 'She and this Rodney Twistlethwaite, a martial arts master, have sucked my Sophie into their conspiracy, and now I'm number one on their hit list,' he said. 'I'll be just the first of thousands of husbands targeted by them.'

He went to the office window and pulled it tight. 'I can feel a bit of a nip in the air,' he said. 'We've got to tighten our security. Where's that little rat Bedsop. He's never around when you want him.'

'You rang, sir?'

It was Bedsop, and he was leaning against the office

wall disguised as a bookshelf.

'How long have you been there?' said Sidney.

'About an hour, I think.'

'What d'you mean, you think?'

'It was so comfortable on the shelf that I nodded off to sleep.'

'Right, we need you wide awake,' snapped Sidney. 'We have a major crisis on our hands. Thousands of lives could be at risk.'

'I'm ready to do or die,' said Bedsop dramatically. 'Who are the enemy?'

'The Japanese.'

'What, all of them?'

'Well, just those belonging to some ancient warrior sect plus any women that they have managed to poison with their propaganda.'

'Who should we target first?'

'Rodney Twistlethwaite.'

'Ah,' said Bedsop. 'That reminds me. I've got good news and bad news for you.'

'Do what?' said Sidney. 'This is no time for good news-bad news jokes.'

'This is not a joke, Mr Bliss,' said Bedsop. 'The good news is that I am now in a position to be able to eliminate Rodney Twistlethwaite from my inquiries.'

'What d'you mean?' challenged Sidney, whose mind was already well advanced on how they were going to make a mass attack on the travel agency in the high street. 'He's been brainwashing my wife.'

'I don't think so, Mr Bliss,' said Bedsop. 'I can now report that she and Mr Twistlethwaite have only ever met once and that was when she called into the travel agency to book a weekend break in Paris.'

Sidney could feel himself coming out in blotches. 'What are you saying to me?' he said, and then answering himself. 'You're telling me that my wife has had nothing to do with this Rodney Twistlethwaite apart from a ten minute meeting in a travel agency?'

'Fifteen minutes actually.'

'So what was all that Japanese martial arts business?' Sidney said. 'The man nearly killed me.'

'Far be it from me to pass an opinion on a matter as personal as this, Mr Bliss,' said Bedsop, 'After all, you are the client and I am only your hired help. But could it be perhaps it had something to do with the fact that you were threatening the perfectly innocent travel agent Mr Twistlethwaite with physical violence?'

'Of course I bleedin' well was,' raged Sidney. 'That was because you had told me that he was plotting with my wife to murder me.'

'A slight case of mistaken identity,' said Bedsop.

Sidney took a wild swing at him but managed only to knock a book off the shelf. Bedsop was now behind him disguised as a wall calendar.

'And dare I ask what the bad news is, wherever you are?' Sidney said, looking around for the man who was driving him insane.

'The bad or good news, according to which way you want to look at it,' said March the twentieth, 'is that I now know who the real Rodney is.'

Sidney sat down, mentally drained. 'All right, let's have it,' he said. 'Which Rodney is my wife seeing?'

140

'Sir Rodney Woodman,' said Bedsop. 'Tonight at seven o'clock.'

'Sir Rodney Woodman?' said Snooper, who was pulling himself back together now that he realised that perhaps his wife was not after all implicated in some great Japanese conspiracy to wipe out the male population of Britain.

'You know this man?' said Sidney.

'Only of him,' said Snooper. 'That's if it's the same Sir Rodney Woodman who publishes the murder books that my wife reads.'

'He publishes murder books?' said Sidney.

'True story stuff,' said Snooper. 'Grizzly accounts of the great murders of the century, and he publishes the memoirs of murderers and the detectives who track them down.'

'Really?' said Bedsop. 'I wonder if he will be interested in commissioning my autobiography. I'm going to call it The Scarlet Pimple. They seek him here, they seek him there. They seek...'

'Shut up!' screamed Sidney in the direction of April the eighteenth where the sound of Bedsop's voice was coming from. 'You've had me on the verge of declaring war on Japan, and now I find that it's not the Japanese who are after me but some flippin' blood thirsty publisher. Well he's about to have the book closed on his little game.'

May the twenty-ninth was snoring. The exhausted Bedsop was fast asleep.

11

I<small>T WAS JUST</small> Sidney's luck that Sir Rodney Woodman turned out to be a former amateur Greco-Roman wrestling champion of the Commonwealth, who had gained a Blue at Oxford and had captained the England team a record ninety-seven times. If he, or the dozy Bedsop, had bothered to look up his entry in *Who's Who* they would have discovered that he listed his hobbies as keep fit, pumping iron and creating new wrestling holds. There in black and white it revealed that he had received his knighthood for services to the sport of wrestling. This was not some pot-bellied, port-quaffing, poufy publisher. This was a man of iron.

Sidney had not learned from his humiliating experience with Rodney Twistlethwaite. It seemed to have deserted his memory that he had not boxed competitively for more than twenty-five years, and he had also forgotten that even at his peak he was not exactly the king of the ring. In fact in his last fight he had become the first boxer ever to finish third in a contest. The judges voted both his opponent and the referee ahead of him.

Yet still it was with a bravado born of false confidence that Sidney confronted Sir Rodney as he approached the front gate of the Bliss home for his evening meeting with the lady of the house.

'Oi mush,' said Sidney with what had become his usual aggressive opening gambit. 'I've got a score to settle with you.'

'I beg your pardon,' said Sir Rodney, instantly on red alert as all his instincts warned him that he had better be prepared to defend himself.

'You *are* Sir Rodney Woodman?' Sidney said, warming up directly in front of him with an Ali shuffle that he had watched The Greatest performing just the previous week on television. The flares of his two-times too big suit polished the pavement over the top of his brogues.

'I am he, but what of it?' Sir Rodney responded, quickly realising that he had some sort of unbalanced man confronting him who was clearly bent on causing trouble.

'You've plotted against me once too often, pal,' Sidney said, now getting a nice sheen of perspiration on his brow ready to launch his opening attack.

Sir Rodney decided that he should try pacifying the obviously disturbed person pirouetting in front of him in what seemed to him a poor imitation of Muhammad Ali. More Ali Baba, he thought. 'Listen my man,' he said in a reasoning tone of voice, 'if you are one of my unsolicited authors to whom I have not returned your manuscript I offer my humble apologies. In fact I am quite prepared to read it now if you have it with you.'

Sidney was in no mood to be reasoned with. 'Listen, old cocker,' he said. 'I know all about you and my wife and how you're planning to get rid of me by burning me to a cinder.'

The laugh that emanated from Sir Rodney's throat should have been a warning to Sidney. It was not a laugh triggered by humour, but more of a scoff that was a preamble to violent action. 'I'm quite prepared to sit down and talk this matter through with you,' he said. 'You are obviously the tormented victim of some delusion.'

'Don't try brain washing me, you murdering swine,' said Sidney, just about to sign his own destruction warrant. 'Put your dukes up.'

Amateur wrestling, a purist sport and certainly not the circus kind you get in the professional ring of heavily muscled forgers, had taught Sir Rodney three main things: 1, Discipline; 2, Self control; 3, Get in first.

He hooked Sidney's shuffling feet from under him with a sweeping movement of his right leg, and then pinned him to the pavement with his own revolutionary hold that he had labelled the Nelson-and-a-half. Many wrestlers had perfected the half Nelson and the full Nelson, but this - as the paralysed Sidney was discovering - was something extra special. It would have taken a contortionist of Harry Houdini standards to have worked a way out of it. With the ease of a seasoned sailor working with rope on a deck, Sir Rodney tied Sidney into a complicated knot that left him writhing on the pavement not knowing his right foot from his left elbow.

Sidney was nothing if not game. Just inches from his face was the inviting sight of an unprotected groin. It was not his usual tactics but on this occasion desperate measures were called for. He opened his mouth and took a great bite, and then screamed with pain as it literally sunk in that he had bitten his own dangly bits.

Sir Rodney was satisfied that he had tamed his

assailant, and got up and prepared to continue on his path to the Bliss front door. He thought perhaps a parting shot was called for. 'Oh by the way,' he said. 'About your book. Don't call us. We'll call you.'

It was only after Sir Rodney had been welcomed inside the Bliss home and the door had closed behind him that Snooper and Bedsop, who had supposed to have been on hand to lend support if needed, dared come out of their hiding place behind next door's hedge.

They picked Sidney up and took him back to the office where they spent the next hour and a half trying to get him unknotted. But they could not get him flat enough to loosen his limbs, and so they took him downstairs to the embalming room and laid him on the slab. Ivor Bodie, used to unravelling limbs locked by *rigor mortis*, applied embalming fluid to make Sidney's legs and arms more supple and then, with the aid of an expertly placed crowbar, freed him at the cost of just a few bruises and abrasions.

As Sidney stepped gingerly to the floor, Bodie shook him by the hand. 'Congratulations, my man,' he said. 'You are only the second person to walk away from that table.'

'Only the second?' said Sidney.

'Yes, there was a case some months ago when we spent two hours embalming a client who had been brought in by ambulance from the local hospital,' he said. 'I was about to place the corpse in the shroud when, imagine my surprise, he sat up and asked for a cup of tea. It transpired that the ambulancemen had made a slight mistake, and had delivered a discharged patient, who had been sleeping, to us and had taken the corpse to the patient's home. His wife said that it was the healthiest she had seen him look. It was a mistake anybody could have made.'

Sidney left Bodie talking away to himself and returned to his office to plan the next campaign in the battle of the sexes.

Sir Rodney reported the unprovoked attack outside the house to Sophie as he opened talks on her book project. 'Oh,' she said, 'don't worry. That will be my Sidney. He's going through a mid-life crisis.'

The publisher recalled how Sidney had screamed when getting his teeth into himself. 'Well I think he has now reached the peak of the crisis,' he said.

Sophie showed him the seven chapters she had written to date, and he read her forty-two thousand words in six minutes flat. 'Sorry it took so long,' he said. 'I'm locked in a legal dispute with the college where I took a speed-reading course. They guaranteed a speed of ten thousand words a minute, but I can't get better than seven thousand.'

'It's still very impressive,' said Sophie. 'It takes me an entire day to read some of the romance novels that I buy.'

There was a pregnant pause that Sophie felt she could measure in fathoms.

'Well,' she said finally, 'what do you think?'

'Think about what?' said Sir Rodney.

'The book, of course,' Sophie said, now feeling embarrassed.

'What book?' said Sir Rodney.

'*Ten Ways to Murder Your Husband*,' said Sophie.

'I'm looking forward to reading it,' said Sir Rodney.

'But you just have,' said Sophie, waving the manuscript under his nose.

'Did I really?' said a puzzled looking publisher. 'Goodness me. Please don't feel offended. I promise you that it is no reflection on what you have written. You now know why I am trying to get my money back from the speed-reading course. I can read with tremendous speed, but I cannot remember a word of it afterwards.'

He smiled. 'I think,' he said, 'that you had better talk me through it so that I know just what I might be buying.'

Bedsop, bugging the conversation from inside the television set in the lounge, nodded his head in agreement. People who silently read documents were a pain in the butt to buggers.

'Right,' said Sophie, 'I shall just summarise the book. This is aimed at the millions of women who at some time or other feel like murdering their husbands.' She added in a small voice to capture the small print: 'It is, of course, a novel and all events and characters are fictitious and bear no relationship to anybody living or dead.'

'Fine,' said Sir Rodney. 'Who are the main characters in the book?'

'Well, there's me... I mean a woman called Sophia Cliss... and her husband, Sidney, cross that out, Rodney, who is the man she is plotting to murder.'

'Careful about the use of the name Rodney,' said Sir

Rodney. 'There are some sensitive people around, and I must warn you that my lawyers will be reading this book very carefully with a view to issuing an injunction.'

'But I can promise you, Sir Rodney, that the character is not based on you.'

'Ah, yes, but you must understand that libel by inference can be just as damaging as direct libel,' he said. 'Just the mere mention of the name Rodney will put my image into the eyes of any reader who knows me. It will only need two of them to contact me, as they surely will once I have tipped them off, and I will take you and your publisher to the cleaners.'

'But you will, I hope, be my publisher,' said a bewildered Sophie.

'Yes, well we will have to see about that. Now that I know that you are dragging my name in the mud I may have to have second thoughts. I must tell you that I am also extremely concerned that you are calling the wife Sophia. Isn't that your name?'

'At birth yes,' said Sophie. 'But nobody ever calls me that.'

'But you could still produce a birth certificate to prove that it is your correct name, and therefore be able to sue yourself and the publishers for thousands of pounds. In fact I am prepared right now to settle out of court if you will accept a payment of five pounds.'

'Five pounds?' said Sophie. 'That sounds a bit derisory to me.'

'Fair enough,' said Sir Rodney. 'But when we get into court I can make the point that we did make you an offer, and the judge will bear that in mind when deciding the extent of the damages.'

'What if I change the name of the characters?'

'Ah, a woman of good common sense,' said Sir Rodney. 'I am glad you suggested that because heaven knows what Sophia Loren might have sued for.'

'How about if the wife is called Clarissa...'

Sir Rodney sucked in his breath. 'Too dodgy,' he said. 'I can't think of a Clarissa off the top of my head but it is a very upper-class type of name. We don't want some Lady Clarissa Bootface coming at us from out of the woodwork at the House of Lords. No. I'm afraid you will need to think again.'

'Um,' said Sophie, thinking again, 'what if I call them Mr and Mrs Smith.'

'Good God, are you mad?' said Sir Rodney, unable to believe his ears. 'Every Mr and Mrs Smith in the world would be looking to sue. It would cost us billions in costs, let alone the damages.'

'Well what if I call them just "S" and "R",' said Sophie with a sudden burst of inspiration.

Sir Rodney shook his head. 'I for one could be instantly identified as R, even if only by inference,' he said. 'Every Roger, Roy, Ronnie, Richard, Raymond, Rastus, Ricardo, René, Robert, Ramon, Rick, Randolph, Rupert, Rolf, Ralph, Rasputin, Reginald...'

'...Robertson, Robinson, Roger...' said a voice from the television as Bedsop found himself lured into the naming game.

'...I've already said Roger,' snapped Sir Rodney. 'Then there's Rudolph, Rudi, Rumplestiltskin, Red,

149

Randall, Rocky, Rocco, Raleigh...'

'Oh come on,' protested Sophie. 'You're not going to tell me that Walter Raleigh is going to sue me.'

'Actually, I was thinking of Raleigh Bowater, an old school chum of mine,' said Sir Rodney. 'He's had a bit of bad luck on the stock exchange recently and would be delighted to get some dosh from you for defaming him in your book. There is, of course, also Rex, Ring, Royce, Rainer, Rai, Remus, Ramus, Rabindranath, Reece, Radoslav, Ramsey...'

'Sir Alf Ramsey would sue me after the way I cheered England to victory in the 1966 World Cup final?' groaned Sophie. 'There's gratitude for you.'

'I was thinking of Ramsey McDonald's descendents,' said Sir Rodney. 'And, of course, we musn't forget Ragner, Renzo, Ross, Rusty, Rauno, Rafer, Romuald, Rodriguez, Rudiger...'

'Hold on,' said Sophie, 'Rudiger is surely covered by Rudi.'

'Yes, I'll accept that point,' said Sir Rodney, 'but what about Reinaldo, Rodolpho, Raphael, Reinhardt, Rutherford, Rohan, Ranji, Ragunath, Rhodes, Roland, Russell, Romeo...'

'...and Juliet,' said Bedsop.

'Turn that dratted television off,' said Sir Rodney. 'I can't think straight with that droning on in the background.'

'Don't worry about that,' said Sophie. 'That's Bedsop. He won't sue.'

'But I'm known to my friends as Ratfink,' said Bedsop. 'They might easily think that "R" is me. Do

150

you want to settle up with me now?'

'I rest my case,' said Sir Rodney. 'You see, even people with nicknames starting with the initial "R" would feel justified in suing you. And goodness knows how many women there are in the world whose name begins with the initial "S".'

'...Samantha...' offered Bedsop for starters.

It was at this point that Sophie's shoe hit the screen, and put the television and Bedsop's recording equipment out of action.

After another three hours of discussion, it was agreed that the two main characters would be called Zuxzg and Xzmazch, with a rider added in small print at the front of the book that these names bore no relationship whatsoever to any aliens who might land within the following millenium, this passage of time to allow for reprints.

They shook hands on a provisional publishing deal, the advance to be dictated by the number of replies Sophie received to the advertisement. Any figure over twenty-seven thousand would guarantee her an advance of thirty thousand pounds. Anything below would bring an advance of fourteen pounds ninety-nine pence. Sir Rodney had checked beforehand that the *Evening Advertiser* had a total circulation of just under eighteen thousand.

'What are the subjects of the last three chapters?' asked Sir Rodney.

'I have definitely decided on Murder by Shooting for chapter eight and Murder by Insecticide for chapter nine,' said Sophie.

'Insecticide?' queried Sir Rodney.

'Yes, that's when Sidney... cross that out... Xzmazch is eaten alive by a moving mountain of killer ants.'

'Very good,' said Sir Rodney. 'And what about the final chapter.'

'I'm torn between two,' said Sophie. 'It could be either Murder by Motor in which Xzmazch is run over by his own car, or Murder by Toothbrush in which Zuxzg loads Xzmazch's toothbrush with twelve hundred volts of electricity.'

'But surely that should come under the Electrocution chapter,' said Sir Rodney. 'We would not want to cheat our readers by doubling up on subject matter, otherwise we could get sued under the trades description act. If we say Ten Ways to Murder Your Husband, it has to be ten ways.'

'Fine, in that case I'll go for Murder by Motor,' said Sophie, 'unless, that is, you prefer a chapter that I thought was perhaps a little too risqué.'

'I'm always happy to take a risk on the risqué,' said Sir Rodney. 'A little spice can help boost sales. What is the subject?'

'The chapter would be called Murder by Hanging.'

'But surely that is covered in the early chapter on strangulation, and I don't see the slightest thing risqué about it.'

'Ah,' said Sophie, 'but Zuxzg would hang Xzmazch by the testicles.'

'Let me have a think about that,' said Sir Rodney, taking a handkerchief from his pocket and wiping his eyes.

Inside the broken television set, Bedsop was crossing his legs. Just how, he wondered, would Sidney Xzmazch react to this?

Back at the office, Snooper was running a lap of honour around the desk after completing his tenth envelope. Sidney had pawned his watch to raise money, and now they were ready to send out their first ten replies which he calculated would generate one hundred pounds in enrolment fees within forty-eight hours.

It was only after they had dropped the stamped envelopes into the post box that Snooper remembered that he had been so intent on typing out the names properly that he had clean forgotten to add the fairly important addresses on the envelopes. This was when Sidney had his first serious doubts about whether their new partnership would work.

The enterprising Bedsop almost saved the day by opening the post box disguised as a postman and retrieving each of the letters, but unfortunately he was savaged by a pack of stray dogs on the way back to the office and all the letters became mutilated during the attack.

Sidney was now reduced to pawning the office typewriter to finance the substitute pack of letters, plus the photo-copied commandments and introductory note and, of course, the request for a ten pounds enrolment fee. It was decided it would be all right for Snooper to write out the envelopes. This he could manage inside an hour, compared to the six days he had taken typing them out.

Mainly because he did not realise it himself, Snooper failed to reveal that he was exceptionally dyslexic and it was left to the post office sorters to try to decipher where the ten letters were bound for: Nloond, Nchtemresa, Ecnslawet, Deargni, Mehubtnroeu, Wek, Roved, Kloopclab, Tupnye and Texret.

As he could no longer afford petrol for his pride-and-joy Jaguar, Sidney pushed the sports car around to the Pleasant Pheasant Plucker just to keep up appearances. He had just enough money for half a pint of bitter, and then suffered an hour-long earache from Ivor Bodie in return for him getting in the next round.

'...and mark my words, the time will come when the Churchill family will get thirteen million pounds for some bits of paper... and there will be a national raffle every week in which people will queue up to buy tickets even though the odds against them winning will be fourteen million to one... and, mark my words, England will not qualify for the next two World Cup finals... '

Sidney had never heard such nonsense in all his life, but had to stand and nod in the right places as the price for his drink. He was looking round the bar feeling sorry for himself when his eyes picked out what appeared to be a party going on in the other bar.

'What's happening back there?' he asked Nancy, while Bodie chuntered on unaware that he had lost his audience.

'It's a farewell party for one of the reporters on the *Advertiser*,' she said. 'That Sheila Blige tart has got herself a job in Fleet Street. I bet she got there on her back.'

154

Sidney silently seethed – which would have been the sort of alliterative skill that had landed Miss Blige her job as an investigative reporter on one of the mass-selling tabloids.

He wondered how he could gain revenge for the way she had used and abused his dating agency, embarrassed poor Bernie Biddle and tried to destroy the livelihood of fairly innocent cemetery gatekeeper Cedric Scratchitt.

Then, staring into the last drops of the beer at the bottom of his glass, he had a sudden brainwave.

It meant employing the doubtful skills of Bedsop, who he could see out of the corner of his eye in his eavesdropping role as a coat stand. He went and stood in front of the small mound of coats and started to speak.

'Listen carefully, Bedsop,' he said. 'I've got a special assignment for you.'

A non-regular customer collecting his coat looked at Sidney as if he was mad. Then he looked at Bodie talking away to himself at the far end of the bar. ''ere, mate, why don't you get together with the bloke at the bar,' he said. 'At least then you'll both have somebody to talk to.'

Sidney ignored him. 'There's a girl reporter holding her leaving party in the next bar,' he said to the coat stand. 'I want you to...'

'Talking to yourself, Mr Bliss?' said a voice behind him. Sidney turned to find Bedsop standing there as himself, with his standard uniform of belted raincoat, bowler hat and rimless glasses.

'I thought you were this coat stand.' Sidney said

sheepishly, feeling a complete fool.

'Oh no,' said Bedsop. 'I see to it that I never use the same disguise twice.'

'Right, listen carefully, James,' he said, and then whispered his instructions into his ear to make sure nobody overheard. He then had to repeat them after Bedsop had removed cotton wool from the ear into which he had been whispering.

Five minutes later Bedsop left the bar holding a sheet of paper on which Sidney had written the words of a song to be sung to the tune of Rudolph the Rednosed Reindeer.

Twenty minutes later a singing gorillagram, a craze that had just been imported from the United States, came and stood directly in front of Sheila Blige, who giggled as he started to sing to her.

Thanks to Nancy, Sidney had a grandstand seat behind the bar and he strained to hear the song that didn't sound a bit like the Rudolph tune to him. Bedsop obviously had tin ears to go with all his other defects, but he made a great gorilla and had even managed to make himself look as big as King Kong.

Sheila, Sheila Laugh-a-lot
Here's a funny twist,
The job you think that you have got
Doesn't even exist.

The letter from the Editor was a fake
Just like so many of your facts,
So this party will now become a wake
Because all you've got is the axe.

Sidney was wondering how Bedsop had managed to change the words as well as the tune when he felt a tap on his shoulder. He turned to find Bedsop standing beside him dressed in a Tarzan outfit. 'I couldn't get a gorilla skin,' he said. 'Will this do?'

Looking back open-mouthed to the scene in the other bar, Sidney watched as the gorilla lifted the still giggling Miss Blige above his shoulders. He then ambled out of the bar with her, and everybody in the pub, apart from the still-talking Ivor Bodie, raced out on to the pavement to see where he was taking her. It was a short journey. He took her to the trough used by the brewery drayhorses and dropped her face first into the cold water.

The giant gorilla then removed his head, and the crying, soaking-wet Miss Blige looked up into the snarling face of Bernie Biddle.

'That will teach you a lesson, Eileen bloody Over,' he said. 'Just for your information, the appointment letter that you think came from Fleet Street and tonight's little ditty were compiled by my girlfriend, Phoebe, who also happens to be the daughter of Cedric, the cemetery gatekeeper you lied about. I 'ope you're less cruel to people when you do one day make it to the Street of Stink.'

Sidney led the applause of the spectators. Even *Advertiser* staff joined in, proving that not everybody approved of Sheila Blige's reporting techniques.

'I told you,' he said to Bernie, 'that Phoebe was perfect for you. But I have to say, that you look better with that gorilla's head on.'

157

Still wearing the suit, Bernie went back into the pub with Sidney and bought him a pint to celebrate the revenge over Miss Blige.

His boss, Ivor Bodie, was still alone at the bar and did not blink as Bernie came into his eyeline dressed as a gorilla.

'Mark my words,' he was saying aloud for anybody's consumption, 'the time will come when divorces will take just three minutes... the Rolling Stones will still be rolling into the next millenium... Cliff Richard will be made a knight... and gorillas will be running the country...'

As Sidney, pushing the Jaguar, returned to a night on the office couch, he wondered about Bodie's prediction that divorces would one day take just three minutes. 'If that unlikely day ever dawns,' he thought to himself, 'there would be no need for undating agencies.'

12

IT TOOK A pantechnicon to deliver the advertisement replies from fed-up wives to the Bliss home, and Sophie had to drive her Mini out of the garage to make room for the hundred and fifty-three sacks of mail. She contacted Sir Rodney Woodman, who sent his entire editorial team to help check through them.

The final letter count was 114,675, which was approximately six times the number of people who bought the *Evening Advertiser*. Sir Rodney himself read through all of the letters in fifteen minutes, close to his top speed, and could remember enough about them to be convinced that he should hand Sophie a thirty thousand pounds advance for the world rights to her book. The tight-fisted Woodman also granted her a miserly 7.5% royalty on the net profits once the advance had been recouped.

Included with every reply sent out were not only the ten commandments but also a request for a ten pound enrolment fee plus an order form for the book, *Ten Ways to Murder Your Husband*.

Not one wife sent back an enrolment fee but every single one of them ordered the book.

As with the advertisement, news of the book travelled by word of mouth, and by the end of the following week 267,985 advance orders had been received. Sir Rodney kicked himself that he had not asked for a book deposit with each order, calculating that the interest alone on a quarter of a million three pound deposits would have quadrupled the previous annual profits of his publishing house.

Sophie refused to cancel her long weekend in Paris, and said that she would write the remaining three chapters on her return. Meantime Sir Rodney's team of worldwide agents were hawking around synopses for the book, and within forty-eight hours deals had been struck with publishers in the United States, Australia, South Africa and every English-speaking country. Translations were ordered in fifty-seven different languages.

Sir Rodney sat down with his calculator and estimated that the first print run would be just over three million copies. Only the Bible, the Koran, the Thoughts of Chairman Mao and Playboy had a bigger run.

Hollywood film producer Stefan Spangross saw a one paragraph outline of the book and immediately flew in to London aboard his private jet, and commanded Sir Rodney to meet him in his suite at the Savoy 'along with da li'l lady who wrote dis epic.'

Sophie put on her best frock and was driven to the Savoy in Sir Rodney's burgundy Rolls Royce. 'Now don't be nervous about this meeting,' Sir Rodney said as they sat in a traffic jam in The Strand for forty-five minutes before his new chauffeur realised he was in a taxi rank. The rimless glasses on the chauffeur's face were the only give-away that it was Bedsop.

'But I am extremely nervous,' said Sophie. 'This is not my scene at all. Sidney has always handled the business side of things. What do I know about book contracts and film deals?'

'Leave it all to Sir Rodney,' said Sir Rodney, patting her comfortingly on the hand, an action noted by the eyes of the chauffeur in the driving mirror. 'These Americans think they can just roll roughshod over us, but they will find that I am a very hard negotiator indeed. We are very much in the driving seat.'

Bedsop checked that he was behind the wheel. 'Begging your pardon, sir,' he said, 'but you are in the passenger seat at the back.'

'You just keep your mind on the road, driver,' said Sir Rodney, making a mental note to get rid of him as quickly as possible. He had already lost them three times during what should have been a forty minute journey from the Bliss home, and he had at one stage tried to drive through the gates of Buckingham Palace in the belief that it was the Savoy Hotel. He had then got caught up in the Changing of the Guard, and he had run over a sergeant major's boot and a guardsman's busby before mounted police had managed to extricate him. Japanese tourists applauded, thinking they were watching a strange English custom. Bedsop doffed his chauffeur's cap in acknowledgement.

As the Rolls moved through Fleet Street thirty minutes earlier, Sophie had the strangest sensation. A down-at-heel hippie with a flare bottom suit that swamped him had stared at her in a mournful, self-pitying manner and for several seconds she felt she was looking into the lovely crumpled face of Sidney. But, no, it could not have been him. He would not have been seen dead in a suit like that.

When the Rolls at last pulled up outside the Savoy, Sophie felt there were enough butterflies in her stomach to fly her upstairs to the Spangross suite without need of the lift. She just wished that Sidney had been at her side. He would have known how to deal with this situation.

Sidney was not too far away from the Savoy. He was just half a mile to the east in the Chancery Lane offices of Rabbitt, Grabbitt and Bankitt, a firm of solicitors that Snooper had recommended to him.

'You obviously can't beat this Sir Rodney chappie physically,' Snooper said, 'so give him a good hiding in court. The British legal system is famous for being the fairest in the world. All the judges say so. I am sure Rabbitt, Grabbitt and Bankitt will be only too happy to represent you. Rabbitt is my favourite cousin, and that is why he has agreed to see you.'

'I have only agreed to see you Mr Fliss...'

'Bliss,' corrected Sidney.

'...because Percival Snooper is, unfortunately, my cousin,' said Rabbitt, looking over the top of his pince-nez at Sidney with undisguised contempt on his face. 'Might I say that our usual clientele know how to dress for an appointment of this nature, and if we should ever get to court with your case I would expect you to wear something, shall we say, more appropriate.'

Sidney pulled George Drinkwater's suit tighter around himself, and tried to untangle the office cat from his flares. 'This is not my usual whistle and flute,' he

162

said. 'All my other gear is in the wardrobe at 'ome. Don't worry about my schmutter, pal. Just give me advice about whether I can sue this Sir Rodney Woodman geezer.'

'How exactly do you feel Sir Rodney has damaged you?' Rabbitt asked, making a note of the time their conversation started.

'Well, 'e's enticed my missus away from me,' said Sidney. 'This 'as caused me great emotional distress and extreme 'ardship, and I ain't 'ad a decent meal in more than two weeks.'

'Enticed you say. How exactly?'

'Well 'e's given 'er a book deal, 'e's driving her round London in a flash Roller, and 'e's advised 'er on 'ow to get rid of me.'

'Rid of you, Mr Cliss...'

'Bliss.'

'What do you mean exactly by "get rid of you"?'

''ow to bump me off.'

'Bump? You mean as in birthday bumps?'

'No, you berk, bump off as in murder.'

'You are saying that Sir Rodney and your wife have conspired to have you murdered?'

'That's right.'

'And what proof have you got?'

'I've had a private eye tailing them and listening in to their conversations. It's all written down in a book.'

'There's written evidence?'

'Yeah, my wife 'as written a book about 'ow she's going to get rid of me with the 'elp of this Sir Rodney geezer.'

163

Rabbitt looked at his watch, noted the time and then stood up.

'I must now terminate this meeting.'

'You're taking the case?'

'No, certainly not.'

'What's the problem?'

'It is simply that I have to inform you that my firm represent Sir Rodney Woodman and his publishing house.'

'You're on 'is bleedin' side too?'

'I wouldn't put it like that, Mr Pliss...'

'Bliss.'

'Let's just say we are on the side of the law, and I cannot be seen to be having divided loyalties. And, of course, Sir Rodney is clearly a man who can pay his bills.'

Rabbitt gave Sidney a hard look, obviously calculating – correctly – that he did not have enough money to pay for a two-piece suit let alone a law suit. He checked the exact time that their meeting had started and finished, switched off the taxi-style meter under his desk and pointed Sidney towards the door.

'If you care to wait downstairs in the reception lobby,' he instructed, 'I will get the writ drawn up that we will be serving on you for gross slander against our client, Sir Rodney Woodman.'

'You must be joking,' said Sidney. 'Stick your writ and your law right up where the sun doesn't shine.'

'So be it, Mr Gliss...'

'Glass,' said Sidney.

'My firm's charges are two hundred pounds an hour

or part therefore. Please pay my secretary on your way out.'

'Pay her for what?'

'For the consulation.'

'You call that a consultation?' Sidney said. 'All you've done is insulted my dress sense and collect evidence on behalf of Sir Rodney What-not. The Berlin Wall will be pulled down before I pay you any bloody money.'

He put his face close to Rabbitt's. 'The law, mush,' he said, 'is an arse.'

'No, the law is an ass,' said Rabbitt.

A victory for Sidney. 'You said it, pal.'

He stormed out of the offices of Rabbitt, Grabbitt and Bankitt, refraining from threatening to punch Rabbitt on the nose just in case he was a black belt in origami or something. Instead he kicked the cat that was asleep furled inside his right trouser leg.

Rabbitt meantime was issuing a writ for slander, and ordered it to be served on a Mr Sidney Glass.

Half a mile to the west in a second floor suite of rooms at the Savoy Hotel Sophie Bliss was so buried in a soft armchair that she was only catching fleeting glimpses of Stefan Spangross as he pace-walked the room, a twelve-inch cigar in his mouth and a small calculator in his hands. Walking after him catching the cigar ash and making notes were a secretary and a personal assistant, both of them with pelmets for skirts and with bosoms that could only have owed their shape and size to the modelling and moulding skill of a Californian plastic surgeon.

165

'Heard about da book and flew right on over,' said Spangross in an accent that was pure, unadulterated Bronx. 'It's gonna take da world by storm, and I'm gonna make it into da greatest ting since Gone wid da Wind. Bigger dan Ben Hur. Wider dan Da Big Country. Deeper dan Twenty Tousand Leagues Under da Sea. Longer dan Da Longest Day. Soundier dan Da Sound of Music. Higher dan High Society. Louder dan Da Guns of Navarone. Scarier dan Psycho. Singier dan Singin' in da Rain. Bondier dan da Bond films. Cassier dan Casablanca. Quoier dan Quo Vadis. Southier dan South Pacific. Thoidier dan Da Thoid Man. More Cleoie dan Cleopatra. Quieter dan All Quiet on da Western Front. Citizenier dan Citizen Kane. More mutinous dan Mutiny on da Bounty. More way out west dan Way Out West, Hunchier dan Da Hunchback of Notre-Dame. More fantastic dan Fantasia. Mickier dan Mickey Mouse. Dumber dan Dumbo. Maltesier dan Da Maltese Falcon. Henrier dan Henry de Fift'. Briefer dan Brief Encounter. More watery dan On Da Waterfront. Sweeter dan Da Sweet Smell of Success. Angrier dan Da Twelve Angry Men. Hotter dan Some Like It Hot. Sandier dan Lawrence of Arabia. Stranger dan Dr Strangelove. Harder dan A Hard Day's Night. Bonnier dan Bonnie and Clyde. More graduated dan Da Graduate. Greater dan Da Greatest Story Ever Told...'

Spangross paused, stood still for five seconds and looked at the chair containing Sophie. 'What's your book called again?'

'*Ten Ways to Murder Your Husband*,' Sophie said. Sir Rodney nodded his agreement, which was his only contribution to date apart from virtually kissing Spangross's feet when they were first ushered into his presence. So much for being in the driving seat.

'Nah, nah, nah, nah, nah,' said Spangross, back to his walking, talking routine. 'Dat might be all right for da book. But we're talking box office here. Ten Ways to Moider Your Husband loses ya most of da men from your audience, and dey're da ones who put deir hands into da pockets of deir pants and pays for da tickets.'

Strange place for pockets, Sophie thought to herself.

'Ya don't get dames going to da movies on deir own. So da Moider Your Husband title is out, out, out. Have ya god dat?'

His petrified personal assistant nodded her head, her bosom bouncing in time with her nod and almost making Sophie seasick.

'Right, now here's where I earn my corn,' he said. 'I'm gonna come up wid a title dat will knock your eyes out. Are ya ready for dis?'

Everybody in the room nodded and waited with baited breath.

Spangross stopped walking and mimed with his right hand, waving the cigar around as if signwriting.

'Da Jazz Singer,' he said.

There was a moment's silence. His two assistants started to applaud. Sir Rodney joined in.

'Uh, but hasn't there been a film called *The Jazz Singer*,' said Sophie quietly. 'Starred Al Jolson, I believe.'

'Is dat so?' said Spangross. 'So you're suddenly a stoodent of da movie business. Damn it. We've god to be original. Let me have anudder brainstorming session wid myself. Dis is why I'm da highest paid prodoocer in da history of Hollywood. It's da ideas I come up wid dat have made me a legend in my own mind.'

He started pacing the room again, his left hand to his temple and his cigar clenched between his teeth looking like a giant frankfurter.

'God it, god it, god it,' he suddenly shouted. 'Dis is IT. Just get your ears around dis...'

Everybody strained to hear.

'Stagecoach,' he announced, as if naming an Oscar winner. 'S-t-a-g-e-c-o-a-c-h.'

There was a silence that could have been measured in cubic feet. Then the two assistants started applauding wildly. Sir Rodney was up on his feet shouting, 'Bravo.'

Spangross beamed around his cigar, and a diamond star twinkled on his expensively capped teeth. 'It's god everyting, ain't it. Stage. Dat makes people tink of da teater, lights, chorus goils, drama, musicals, fright and big-time management. And Coach. Exciting transport, da sportsfield, da old, much loved coach who showed da poor baseball playing kid how to get on da right side of da tracks, da wild west wid Injuns firing flaming arrows at da brave guy riding shotgun - John Wayne of course - and da start of da railways in da good old U. S. of A., and da rail coaches being attacked by da James Boys, but we mustn't make dem all bad because da public have grown to love deir legend, so maybe we can have dem rescuing da sports coach from a coach surrounded by hordes of war-painted, uh, not red injuns, dat's become taboo... we'll have war-painted eskimos, no dat'll be bad for business in Alaska... god

168

it, war-painted Cossacks, provided da Cold War is still on, if not we'll make 'em war-painted aliens, nobody's god around to campaigning for deir rights, yet...'

Sophie had her hand up, and it took Spangross some time to spot it in the depths of the armchair.

'Ya trying to distract my attention, lady?' he said. 'Dat's a dangerous ting to do when I'm really pumping. Could blow a brain socket. What da hell is it now?'

'Uh, I think you'll find,' said Sophie timorously, 'that John Wayne starred in the original version of *Stagecoach*.'

'Jeez, it's so damned hard to be original dese days,' said Spangross, puffing harder on his cigar until the room was suddenly enveloped in blue smoke. 'It was all right for dose guys like D.W. Griffith and Mack Sennett to be original. Dere was a whole virgin desert of ideas for dem to work on. Hollywood has become pretty crowded since den. It ain't easy to find somethin' that ain't been done already. But Stefan Spangross didn't get to da top of da heap by being beat by no movie title. I've god a million of 'em, ain't dat right guys and dolls?'

'A million of 'em Mr Spangross,' chorused the dolls.

'Yes, quite, a million Mr Spangross,' said Sir Rodney.

'What dis prodoocer needs is a good ol' cup of piping hot black coffee to wash down one of my special pills to help da old brain juices flow.'

The personal assistant, the secretary and Sir Rodney all collided as they raced as one for the telephone to call room service. While they were picking themselves up, Sophie picked up the extension alongside her armchair and ordered a pot of coffee.

169

Within five minutes there was a rat-tat on the door. 'Room service 'ere,' came a distinctive young Cockney voice.

Spangross lifted his arms to the heavens like a man saved at a Billy Graham crusade. 'Tank you God,' he said to the ceiling. Tank you, tank, you tank you. I've god it, I've god it, I've god it, by George Washington, I've god it.'

'He's got it, he's got it, he's got it,' squealed the personal assistant and the secretary, managing to sound like the Supremes backing Diana Ross.

Sir Rodney threw up his arms. 'He's got it. By George, he's got it.'

A waitress, blonde, pretty, twenty, came in carrying the coffee on a tray.

'Say dat line again, goilie,' Spangross said to the waitress, who looked over her shoulder to see who he was referring to.

'You,' he said, pointing his cigar at the waitress. 'Say dat line you said when you knocked at da door.'

'Is this some kind of wind up?' the waitress said, blushing and looking for a hidden camera. 'This ain't that Canada Camera show, is it? All I bleedin' well said was "Room service 'ere".'

'Don't ya luv it,' said Spangross clapping his hands together.

The dolls and Sir Rodney all clapped along, and Sophie wondered if they were about to break into Baby Love.

'Have you ever wanted to be in pictures, goilie?'

'Who me?' said the waitress. 'Nah. It ain't my cup of

tea. I'm 'appy as I am, fanks very much.'

'But I'm casting a new movie and I can make you a star,' said Spangross, inspired without need of the coffee and the pill. 'I can see it now. Young Cockney waitress woiking in a posh London hotel. She's spotted by this high powered movie prodoocer who loins her to speak proper, and he takes her to Hollywood and she stars in the movie that sweeps the Oscars. He calls da movie...'

'My Fair Lady?' said the waitress, laughing with her hands cupped to her face. 'Ooh, you ain't arf a caution, mister, make no mistake. That's already been done that 'as with Audrey 'epburn, when it obviously should 'ave been Julie Andrews in the part.'

Spangross chewed heavily on his cigar. 'Anudder stoodent of da movies,' he said. 'Dat's all I need. I'm surrounded by dem. As it happens, baby doll, I was not gonna call it dat at all. No, my title is, just wait for this sugar, Mary Poppins.'

'Wow, Mary Poppins,' chorused the Supremes.

'Sounds a corker to me,' said Sir Rodney.

There was a new bounce in Spangross's stride as he resumed his walk. 'I'll have you playing da lead alongside dat distinguished Cockney actor Dick van Dyke,' he said, looking at the waitress through a make-believe camera lens.

She burst out laughing again. 'That's been done 'n' all,' she said. 'And what a load of old crap it were. That Dick van Dyke sounded about as Cockney as Omar Shariff.' She did a quick take off of his accent. 'Oi've just swept the chiminey, Miss Porpins, and nah oi'm gonna take the kids for a roide ta see some of the soights

171

of ol' Lundin tarn.'

'God, this kid's great,' said Spangross. 'That's authentic Cockney. What's your name sweetheart?'

'Molly,' she said, 'Molly Shufflebottom.'

'Jeez, well we'll soon get dat changed. I can see it now. Raquel Shufflebottom in Goodbye Dolly. Whaddya tink, babe?'

'I fink you've lost your marbles, mate,' said Molly. 'Me and me husband, Pete, are expecting our second baby five months from now and I wouldn't give my family up for all the tea in China.'

With that she turned and swept out of the room. Only Sophie applauded. Spangross shrugged. 'Some you win, some you lose. Dat's da attitood dat's got me where I am today.'

He took a quick mouthful of coffee and washed down a pill. 'Now den, where was we? Ah, yeah. A title. What was your book called again?'

'*Ten Ways to Murder Your Husband*,' said Sophie.

'Yeah, dat's quite catchy,' said Spangross. 'Might have to tink of anudder woid for Moider, and da Husband bit may have to go. But I just love Ten Ways to... It could be da start of a whole new series. Ten Ways to Sing da Star Spangled Banner... Ten Ways to Impeach A President... Ten Ways to Make Wall Street Crash... Ten Ways to Break Outta Alcatraz... Ten Ways to Tell Your Mamma You're Sorry dat ya Forgot Her Boithday But I'm Such A Busy Busy Boy in Hollywood Dese Days...'

He stopped his walkie-talkie perambulation, and dabbed at his eyes with a handkerchief.

172

'For now,' he said, quickly getting back into his stride, 'we'll settle for a working title of Ten Ways to Blank Your Blank. Now den, writer lady, tell me who are da main characters.'

Sophie took a deep breath before replying. 'Zuxzg and Xzmazch,' she said, 'a typically English surburban couple.'

'Ya've godda be kidding me,' Spangross said, almost biting through his cigar. 'What sort of stoopid clodbrain came up wid dat combination?'

Sir Rodney proudly raised an arm.

'Nah, nah, nah, nah,' he said. 'Dis ain't da dusty, cobwebbed publishing world in which ya put books out for prestige radder dan profit. In my business ya've godda tink box office, box office, box office. Right, for a start we'll name da characters Richard and Pat. Dat's god a nice Presidential feel about it. Dat'll go down well in Washington, and if dis Watergate business gets any bigger we can call dem Richard and Pat Gatewater. Get da connection? V-e-r-y commercial. Spangross strikes again. Dat pill is really gedding to woik. So whaddya tink? Ten Ways to Blank Your Blank, the true story of the loves and lives of Richard and Pat Gatewater.'

He waited for some reaction from his troops. His two assistants duly applauded, and Sir Rodney punched the air. Spangross looked at Sophie.

'Well? What does da author tink, or are ya one of dose typically precious writers who jealously guard every word as though it's your own,' he said, more in an accusing than enquiring way. 'Well I'll tell ya, lady, ya won't last five minutes in Hollywood wid dat

173

attitood. All ya've godda do is come up wid da original idea, da book and da screenplay and den leave da rest to us. We'll quickly improve on every syllable and leave no idea of yours untouched and unplundered. Den when da Oscars roll in we'll take all da glory, and, to show we are fair, give ya all da credit if and when da films bomb. Writers. Huh. Dey're just cabs on a rank. One goes, anudder quickly follows. Anybody who can spell can write. But how many people can prodooce? How many great prodoocers do ya know, lady?'

Sophie shrugged. She couldn't think of a single one that she knew personally, but it was definitely one less than he thought.

'Dere ya are, ya see,' he said. 'We're a breed apart. We don't grow on trees. We're God's gift to mankind. Widout us Hollywood would be just da wood widout da holly. I just taut of dat. Did you geddit? Da wood widout da holly.'

His secretary noted it down while his personal assistant and Sir Rodney applauded.

'Right,' he said, 'all we've godda do now before we wrap dis deal up is come up wid da stars. Richard has godda be a sex symbol, somebody who makes da goils swoon. God it, god it, god it. It's godda be Rock Hudson.'

Sophie was impressed. 'Wow,' she thought, 'sex on legs.'

Spangross looked at Sophie. 'Well? Whaddya tink?'

'Well he doesn't quite look like my Sidney,' she said, 'but I must agree he would have what you call box office appeal. There's not a lady in the world who

174

would not like to have his arms around her. Not unless they've got strange tastes, that is.'

'Good, good, good,' said Spangross, pointing his cigar at Sophie like a conductor's baton. 'Da lady loins good. Now she's tinking box office. We'll have you into da ways of Hollywood in no time. Swinging parties, perfectly mixed martinis, maybe just a li'l narcotics but not enough to become hooked, skinny dipping in da pool at midnight, perhaps a little surgery to take an inch or two off dat nose, your own black maid or maybe dese days you'd better tink Oriental or Wetback, a bronzed young stud fixed up in his own apartment dat you pays for outta da royalties, a limo with blacked-out windows dat stretches for ever, a room at da back of your mansion for your li'l ol' mudder, like I've promised mine but have not yet got round to it...'

He stopped and dabbed at his eyes again, but was quickly back on his walking-talking tour of the suite.

'Now der's just da leading lady to cast and den we can get on wid drawing up contracts. Now it's too much of a Hollywood cliché to match Rock Hudson wid Doris Day. Well I ain't got a cliché in my bones. No, sur. Wad I have in mind will blow your minds. Are you ready for dis.'

His cigar was signwriting again.

'Ten Ways To Blank Your Blank starring Rock Hudson and...'

He paused, knowing that he had his audience in the palm of his hand.

'...Rock Hudson and Shoiley Temple.'

The applause from his sycophantic staff brought

175

complaints about the noise in the royal suite to the Savoy reception desk. Sir Rodney did not help by leaping up and chanting like an American cheerleader.

Sophie's hand was up, bringing a dampner to the party proceedings.

'Just a minute,' said Spangross with heavy sarcasm coating his voice. 'Da writer wants to pud in her two cents worth.'

'It's just that, to use your terminology,' said Sophie, 'Shirley Temple does not seem to have box office pulling power.'

'Whad is dis broad talking about?' said Spangross, shaking his head. His two assistants and Sir Rodney shook theirs in support.

'Shoiley Temple was da biggest box office sensation Hollywood has ever known in da years leading up to da war,' said the producer, puffing smoke signals that revealed he was less than happy with 'da writer'.

'But that was more than thirty years ago,' said Sophie.

'Exactly,' said Spangross in triumph.

'Exactly,' chorused his two assistants and Sir Rodney, who had a contract out ready to be signed.

'Can't you see da public being just desperate to find out whad she's grown up like?' said Spangross, his eyes alight with dollar bill signs. 'Imagine da worldwide publicity we get when Rock runs his hands through dat bubble-coil hair of hers.'

'It's hardly likely to be bubbles now,' said Sophie.

Spangross tutted. His two assisants and Sir Rodney tutted on cue like percussionists.

'Ya see ya just don't know how Hollywood woiks,' he said. 'For da shots of da bubbly hair being stroked by Rock we'll bring in what's known as a stand-in. And for da long-range shots, Shoiley will wear a bubble-coil wig. Just tink of da soundtrack rights alone.'

He tapped away on his calculator like a demented Horowitz at the keyboard.

'Rock and Shoiley singing a dooet on Animal Crackers,' he said. 'Jeeze, we're talking zillions. Rock can mime, and we'll get Sinatra or Andy Williams to do da dubbing. And just tink of da climax. We can have Shoiley on a torpedoed liner in da middle of a storm in da Atlantic. She's a dancer on da boat. So here we have da ultimate in a musical disaster epic. Rock can fly in and rescue her in his own twin-engine 'plane and as he hooks her off da deck of da sinking liner dey can dooet on Da Good Ship Lollypop. Closing titles over Shoiley and Rock in a clinch, wid the water dripping off her clinging dress. We can cut in a shot dere of Ursula Andress coming out out of da water in Dr No. Jeez, we're talking a clutch of Oscars here.'

The two assistants were applauding and crying at the same time. Sir Rodney was blowing his nose, making a hooter sound that Spangross acknowledged with a bow.

He looked at Sophie. 'I'm quite speechless,' she said.

'Good,' said Spangross. 'Da emotion of it all has god to you. Dat shows you've god heart. And dat's whad you need most of all in Hollywood. Heart. Miles and miles and miles of heart.'

He clutched at his wallet.

The Supremes hugged each other, their mascara

running in black rivers down their painted faces. Sir Rodney, his cheeks tear stained, stood with the contract poised for signing.

'Not just yet, Sir Rodney,' said Sophie. 'I want to go away and think about this.'

'Think about what?' said Sir Rodney.

'Whad?' said a stunned Spangross. 'Da goil's crazy. She wants to tink about a contract dat's gonna be woith billions, zillions even when I ged da necessary backing for da epic. Zillions.'

'Zillions,' chorused the Supremes.

'Let me talk to you about this after my break in Paris,' she said. 'I've got a clear picture in my mind of how I want the book to develop, and I shall give you, Sir Rodney, first refusal when I return home next Tuesday.'

'Now hold on lady,' said Spangross. 'What about *my* first refusal on da film rights?'

'You can have them, of course,' said Sophie. 'But don't expect a book that quite ties in with all the garbage you have been spouting here this afternoon.'

The prodoocer nearly choked on his cigar. The Supremes were silenced. Sir Rodney wrestled his hands in grief.

Across the suite of rooms the curtains pulled themselves together and applauded. Bedsop fully approved of Sophie's stand.

She wondered what Sidney would have made of it all.

13

THE GUN sticking in Sidney's back was a .38 Browning revolver last fired during the Normandy Landings of 1944. He went cold with fear as it dawned on him that Sophie had decided on Murder by Shooting to get him out of her life for good.

Whoever had been hired as his killer was keeping himself well hidden behind a Mickey Mouse mask and with the brim of a large, dark trilby pulled down over his eyes. He had been hiding in the office waiting for Sidney to return from a traumatic lunchtime meeting with a tearful Percival Snooper.

'I can't go on... I can't go on,' Snooper had told him in his highly emotional manner, whining through a nose as pinched as a baby's bum. 'I am a broken man. The strain is killing me. Look at me. I've become a wreck. A snivelling, grovelling caricature of a once proud and self-assertive master of all I surveyed.'

Sidney was embarrassed as he stood at the saloon bar of the Pleasant Pheasant Plucker. 'Get off your knees and stop making a fool of yourself,' he hissed. 'What are you on about?'

Snooper realised that, even by his standards, he was being a little over-dramatic. He pulled himself together as effortlessly as if drawing curtains, and talked rationally and calmly. 'I'm afraid I have to tell you that I am giving up,' he said.

'Giving up what?' said Sidney.

'The Undating Agency... our partnership... the one-sided battle... celibacy...'

'You mean...'

'Yes, I'm going home to Patsy,' Snooper said. 'Sorry, Sidney, but the pull is too strong. I know it means breaking every one of our commandments, but I can't last another day without her. You'll have to soldier along on your own.'

'Alone?' said Sidney. 'You seem to forget that I've got ten thousand punters pledged to supporting the aims and ambitions of The Undating Agency.'

'But we've not had a single reply from the first ten on the shortlist,' said Snooper, 'and I'll tell you why. We've been beaten by that counter-attack from the wives. The masterstroke was their tenth commandment.'

'What,' said Sidney, '"Thou shalt not allow him to have any nookie"?'

'That's the one,' said Snooper. 'It has brought the starved husbands of Britain to their knees begging for forgiveness. I'm sorry, Sidney. But you're now on your own.'

As Snooper walked out of the pub for a passionate reunion with Patsy, Ivor Bodie was alone at his corner of the bar. '... Mark my words, the time will come when more couples will live together than get married,' he said aloud to himself. 'I'm telling you that the end of the world as we know it is nigh... the Royals will lead the divorce revolution, just you wait and see... even the Queen's position will be put in jeopardy by a couple of mad cows... there will be women priests, gay vicars and men will marry each other... there will be a terrible disease that will wipe out thousands and nobody will buy Liberace's piano stool... Australia will become a Republic... and one day footballers will earn ten thousand pounds a week...'

If he could have afforded it, Sidney would have cried into his beer. But he had drained his one half-pint glass and walked out in a deep depression rather than listen to any more from the speaking clock. Then, just to make his day, he had returned to the office to be jumped from behind by the gunman.

'What are you going to do with me?' he said over his shoulder to the man with the gun and the contract.

'I have strict instructions,' he said in a voice that sounded familiar to Sidney. 'Just do as you're told or else...'

It then came to Sidney whose voice it was. It was a perfect imitation of Mickey Mouse.

The gun pressed into the small of his back, Sidney was forced downstairs. As they stepped out of the funeral parlour, Bernie Biddle was just shutting the back of the hearse after loading his latest client for the start of the final journey.

Sidney winked at him, and pulled a face to draw attention to the assassin at his back. Bernie just waved. 'Watcher, Mr Bliss,' he said. 'Hello Mickey.'

Then he opened the passenger door of the hearse and helped Mickey bundle him into the front seat.

With Bernie at the wheel and Mickey sitting alongside him with the gun in his ribs, Sidney was driven slowly away.

'Why, Bernie?' he said. 'Why have you turned

181

against me?'

'It's for your own good,' said Bernie, his eyes on the road ahead. 'And anyway, Phoebe said she would break off our engagement if I did anything to encourage The Undating Agency.'

'Sophie is behind this, isn't she?' Sidney said to Mickey.

'Just do as you're told,' he repeated in his high-pitched voice as the hearse pulled up outside Sidney's home. 'Wait here, Bernie. We'll be five minutes.'

Sidney was led up the garden path, perhaps literally, and Mickey opened the front door with a key that had been left under the mat. He took Sidney upstairs to the main bedroom.

'All right,' said Mickey, flourishing the gun, 'Get your clothes off.'

What on earth was Mickey Mouse going to do to him, Sidney wondered. He was about to put up a fight for his life and his honour when he noticed that a Prince of Wales check suit, a freshly ironed shirt and a change of underwear and socks had been left lying on the bed.

This would have been his dying wish — not to have breathed his last in George Drinkwater's appallingly bad taste, ill-fitting suit.

Once dressed at his best and in what most people would have described as questionable taste, Sidney felt like a new man. 'All right, Mickey,' he said. 'Now do your worst.'

Deep inside, Sidney was feeling good. He sensed something pleasant was about to happen to him, and he had not been the slightest bit taken in by Bedsop's disguise. Well, except perhaps for the first ten minutes or so of the charade. He had guessed it was all just an elaborate leg pull when Bernie had spoken to a mourner sitting in the back of the hearse alongside the coffin. 'Don't worry,' he had said to the mourner. 'I'll get us to the crematorium in good time, just as soon as we've got rid of Mr Bliss.'

That was way over the top, and Sidney did not fall for it for a minute. He played along with their game as Mickey led him back to the hearse.

'Okay, Bernie,' Mickey ordered. 'Put your foot down. We've got less than an hour.'

Bernie took the instruction too literally, and they had been travelling for just ten minutes along a dual carriageway when there was the sound of a police car siren. They were waved down and ordered to pull into a lay-by.

'Not a word about the gun,' Mickey hissed, 'or we'll all get it.'

The police driver walked slowly to the driver's window, making a note of the registration number on the way.

'Where's the fire?' he said with a sarcasm that was wasted on Bernie.

'What fire?' said Bernie.

'The one you're obviously chasing.'

'We're not going to a fire, officer,' he said. 'We're going to a funeral.'

The police constable looked around at the passengers, and was particularly taken by Mickey Mouse.

'Whose funeral?' he said. 'Minnie's?'

'We don't use Minis,' said Bernie. 'Only Rollers and limos.'

'The deceased was a leading member of the British branch of the Mickey Mouse Club,' said Mickey, now in a deeper voice that, Sidney thought, showed off Bedsop's remarkable range.

'Okay,' said the officer, satisfied. 'I'll let you off with a caution this time. Just watch your speed. Otherwise it will be *your* funeral.'

As Bernie drove off at an acceptable forty miles an hour, the mourner in the back laughed. 'Goodness me, this is the most exciting day of Uncle Stanley's life,' he said in a voice that Sidney instantly recognised.

''ow d'you do that?' he said to Mickey.

'Do what?'

'Throw your voice like that.'

'Like what?'

'To make it sound as if it came from back there.'

'What, back here?' said the mourner.

Sidney looked over his shoulder into the almost smiling face of Bedsop.

'What are you doing back there?' Sidney said, doing a double take.

'I'm keeping my Uncle Stanley company,' said Bedsop. 'He's being cremated at two o'clock.'

'My condolences,' said Sidney, his mind racing.

'Oh, this is no time for grieving,' said Bedsop. 'Uncle Stanley had had the time of his life before kicking the bucket at ninety-one. He would want us to celebrate his having been here rather than mourn his passing.'

184

Sidney looked at Mickey. 'So who the 'eck are you?'

He removed his mask. 'Nice to meet you again,' said Sir Rodney Woodman, shaking Sidney warmly by the hand. The strength in the grip reminded Sidney all too vividly of the day he got knotted.

'What is all this?' said Sidney.

'Sorry about the complex plot,' explained Sir Rodney. 'We just felt that if we approached you and said that Sophie wanted to see you you might have refused.'

'And that,' said Bernie, 'would have ended any chance of a second honeymoon.'

'The Mickey Mouse mask was my idea,' said Bedsop.

'That figures,' said Sidney. 'But what's this about a second 'oneymoon?'

'You'll see in a few minutes,' said Sir Rodney. 'By the way, I'm sorry I had to tie you in knots the other day. But you did rather ask for it with your belligerent behaviour.'

'Well wouldn't you have been belligerent if you had thought somebody was trying to take your wife away from you?'

'Actually, old boy, I would be rather delighted. I just happen to be one of the husbands who replied to your advertisement.'

'So you've not been 'aving an affair with my Sophie?' said Sidney.

'Goodness me, no. I've got my own little bit on the side, thank you very much. My house editor, actually. Just my type, you know.'

The hearse pulled up outside Terminal One at Heathrow Airport. While Bernie and Bedsop were saying an emotional farewell to Sidney, a traffic warden was planting a parking ticket on the windscreen. 'Uncle Stanley must have known that was going to happen,' said Bedsop. 'When he was put in his coffin he had two fingers raised. And it wasn't the victory sign.'

Sophie was waiting at the British European Airways check-in desk for Paris.

She kissed Sidney as casually as if she had seen him at breakfast that morning. 'Hello, darling,' she said. 'You're just in time for the flight.'

'Hello soppy Sophie,' whispered Sidney, trying hard not to be soppy himself as tears welled in his eyes.

She then kissed Sir Rodney lightly on the cheek. 'Thank you Sir Rodney for getting him here,' she said. 'You're a petal.'

'I'm just an old romantic,' said Sir Rodney. 'But I am also very commercial, and I still want first refusal on that book.'

'What book?' said Sidney.

'I'll tell you all about it on the plane,' said Sophie. 'We've got a lot of talking, and a lot of loving, to do.'

Sidney's beam lit up the air terminal. 'Sounds just the job to me,' he said.

Sir Rodney waved them off, and shouted after them as they entered the departure lounge. 'I don't think Rock Hudson and Shirley Temple are quite right,' he bellowed through cupped hands. 'You two look more suited to Tracy and Hepburn to me.'

An airport worker alongside Sir Rodney shook his head. 'No, mate,' he said. 'I reckon they're a dead ringer for Hattie Jacques and Sidney James.'

On the flight, Sophie explained why she had arranged this second honeymoon.

'The fact that you were ready to fight first Rodney Twistlethwaite and then Sir Rodney proved to me that deep down you had the same feelings for me that I have for you,' she said. 'I've always loved you Sidney Bliss, and I always will.'

Sidney's crumpled face loosened into a smile, but then clouded for a second.

'But what about all these plots to murder me?'

'That was all a flight of fantasy,' she said. 'I've written this novel called *Ten Ways to Murder Your Husband*, and it helped me get rid of my frustration and anger every time you made a play for one of our lonely heart clients.'

'It was all in my mind then?'

'In both our minds,' said Sophie. 'That's the way it's got to be. Husbands and wives must allow each other their fantasies and their daydreams if their marriage is to survive.'

'You sound just like a marriage counsellor.'

'That's what I'm going to suggest as our next business venture,' said Sophie. 'The Blissful Marriage Guidance Agency. We've both got proof that there are thousands of couples out there in need of guidance. Separation and divorce is not the answer. Togetherness is the only way forward. All that rubbish about the single people getting all the loving. Don't you believe it. They are the real lonely ones.'

'So what happens to the book now?' said Sidney.

187

'I've got to make a decision about that when we get back from Paris,' she said. 'I've had all sorts of offers for the rights, including a thirty thousand pounds advance from Sir Rodney.'

'Thirty grand?' said Sidney, so loudly that the already agitated passenger walking down the aisle nearly jumped out of his dark green safari suit. He turned and pointed a six-cylinder Colt pistol last fired in the battle of the Bay of Pigs at Sidney's head.

'Thees plane will change course for Cuba,' he shouted, 'or thees gringo will be the first to die.'

'But there won't be enough fuel, you fool,' said Sidney, too elated by his reunion with Sophie to be frightened. And anyway, he knew a Bedsop disguise when he saw one.

'I'm telling you that I keel you if this 'plane doth not land in Havana,' the Cuban said. 'Viva Castro. Viva la Revolución.'

'Listen, mush,' said Sidney, playing along to keep Bedsop happy. 'I'll tell you once more. We don't have enough fuel, you fool.'

'Enough fool?' said the heavily perspiring Cuban, his finger tightening on the trigger. 'Don't call me a fuel, you Engleesh peeg.'

'But I'm telling you,' said Sidney as casually as if talking to a man at the bar, 'that a London to Paris flight would not have enough fuel on board to reach Barcelona, let alone Cuba.'

'Thees is a London to Parees flight?' said the Cuban.

'That's right,' said Sidney.

'Prove it,' said the revolutionary, his dark green safari

188

suit now blackening with sweat.

'We're going there on our second honeymoon,' said Sophie, holding the hotel brochure in front of him. 'Look, here's our hotel.'

'Oh, sheet,' said the Cuban. 'I thought thees was the London to Miami flight.'

Sidney calmly took the gun off him. 'Very good, Bedsop,' he said. 'Now sit down and show some respect to your late Uncle Stanley.'

The weeping Cuban was led away by two cabin staff and the co-pilot.

Sophie kissed Sidney's leathery old face, and the rest of the passengers stood and applauded.

But Sidney, the hero, did not hear them. Realising that it was not Bedsop, he had dropped off into a faint.

British European Airways, seeking publicity for when they became British Airways the following year, insisted on picking up the tab for Sidney and Sophie's second honeymoon. He collected another thousand pounds from the *Advertiser* for his own exclusive story of how he disarmed the Cuban revolutionary, who had not been informed by his travel agent that there was now a direct flight service to Havana.

The interview was by Sheila Blige, whose imagination ran even wilder than in her cemetery orgy exposé. Even Sidney had difficulty believing that he had wrestled a machine gun and a machete off six hand-grenade carrying Cubans before landing the plane after the pilot had been knocked unconscious. But the story won Sheila the Scoop of the Year prize and clinched her a

189

Fleet Street job. This time she went to bed with the Editor to make sure that it was not a hoax. She later reported to friends that it had been like making love to a corpse.

Sophie shut herself away for a week on her return from Paris, and carried out major surgery on her book.

When she handed it to Sir Rodney, he turned pale. 'But this has no commercial value whatsoever,' he said. 'I couldn't *give* this to Stefan Spangross.'

For a start, Sophie had changed the title. It was now called *Ten Ways to Love Your Husband*.

There were, of course, ten chapters:

LOVE BY TOUCH

LOVE BY FEELING

LOVE BY GIVING

LOVE BY REMEMBERING

LOVE BY SHARING

LOVE BY UNDERSTANDING

LOVE BY TALKING

LOVE BY AGREEING

LOVE BY FORGIVING

LOVE BY LOVING

'I'll come back with some sort of an offer,' said Sir Rodney, 'but don't expect it to run to four figures.'

He took the manuscript to an editorial conference, and tossed it on to the table. 'What on earth are we going to do with this?' he said. 'Anybody got any ideas?'

It was the house editor who came up with the solution that night in bed as she lay in Sir Rodney's strong arms.

The book went on sale with a beautifully-shot photograph of a naked couple laying together on black, silk sheets. The book was re-titled *Carry On Loving*, and became a best-seller.

Stefan Spangross bought the film rights for two hundred thousand dollars, and got a clutch of Oscar nominations. His film version was called *Stagecoach On the River Kwai* and starred Rock Hudson and Lassie.

With the money earned from the book, Sophie cleared off all their debts and even made the taxmen happy.

Then, on the same day that Bernie Biddle and Phoebe Scratchitt married, Sophie and Sidney invited any couples who cared to join them to repeat their marriage vows at the same ceremony. The church was jammed to capacity, and a loudspeaker was fitted up to relay the service to the thousands of couples outside.

Inside the church, Sophie and Sidney were overjoyed to see James and Patsy Snooper, Sir Rodney and Lady Woodman, George Drinkwater and Nancy, James and Jemima Bedsop, Molly and Peter Shufflebottom, Sheila Blige and her new Editor, and photographer Ralph and Rodney Twistlethwaite — a double-take here, yes Ralph and Rodney — vowing to carry on loving each other 'til death do them part.

Back in the almost deserted saloon bar of the Pleasant Pheasant Plucker, the inexhaustible Ivor Bodie was holding court. '...and, mark my words, the day will come when everybody will realise that arguing and fighting does not make sense and they will all *carry on loving...*'

Nobody took a blind bit of notice of him.

191

DON'T MISS THE OTHER HILARIOUS TITLES IN THIS **CARRY ON** SERIES

And don't forget that all the *Carry On* classics are also available on the Cinema Club video label, and distributed by VCI, price £4.99 each. Watch the videos, read the books... and *Carry On laughing*.